"I think we should do it in the air," I say.

The shower goes off. The curtain slides open. "What did you say?"

I hand him the towel. "Do it in the air."

"Do it in the air." He says it slow, like he's tasting every letter. Then he smiles and wraps his big wet self around me. "We're going to do it in the air."

"Actually," I say, "I was thinking that, too."

He frowns. "Huh?"

"Never mind." I take his towel and drape it over his head.

"But how exactly," he says, "are we going to *do* it in the air?"

"Don't ask me," I say, walking out of the bathroom. "It's time for *you* to come up with some of the answers."

DON'T LOOK DOWN

Tima Smith

BALLANTINE BOOKS • NEW YORK

Copyright © 1996 by Tima Smith
Excerpt from *Buck Naked* by Joyce Burditt copyright © 1996 by Joyce Rebeta-Burditt

http://www.randomhouse.com

Library of Congress Catalog Card Number: 95-95085

ISBN 0-345-39677-4

Manufactured in the United States of America

First Edition: July 1996

10 9 8 7 6 5 4 3 2 1

For Peter and David with love . . .
And A.E., for his constancy, his support, his knowledge.

CHAPTER ONE

I'm standing there half asleep, sipping a cup of coffee and listening to a guy in dreadlocks sing "Dream a Little Dream of Me," when I spot the seven-forty nearing the station. For a second I think about taking the next train, waking up a little, finishing the song and the coffee. But then there's the meeting with Mr. Minican at nine-fifteen. The meeting where he's expecting to see the drawings for the spring line. Not sketches, Amanda, I tell myself. Drawings. With details, styles, specifications. A woman reading a paper glances up at me, which makes me wonder if I just said all that out loud.

The train squeals to a stop, the doors slide open, I take one final gulp and toss the cup into a bin. Then I toss a dollar into the open guitar case, and, for some reason, the wink he gives me knocks me off balance. That makes the second time today. And I've only been awake for a little over an hour.

I slide into a window seat and consider another reason why this day has me on edge. Not that it's something you particularly go out of your way to commemorate, the date you got divorced. But it ends up

1

being there anyway. Leaping out at you from the calendar while you're standing there in your bathrobe totally unprepared, holding down the button on the toaster so it can't pop right back up again after only three seconds.

I lean my umbrella against my leg and pull my sketchbook and pencil out of my bag.

"Excuse me." His elbow bumps my arm as he sits down.

"It's all right," I say. We smile at each other briefly. Out of the corner of my eye I recognize the shoes, Gucci. And the attaché, expensive. He's occasionally on the seven-forty. But so far the only contact we've had has been visual. And unconvincingly accidental.

"Lousy weather," he says.

"Terrible. This rain seems endless."

"They did say it might clear out today."

"I think they said that yesterday, too."

"Guess they figure eventually they have to be right."

We smile at each other again, and I open my sketch pad to the page I was working on last night before I traded it in for a bowl of popcorn and Sidney Sheldon.

I feel him eyeing the drawings. "Art student?" he asks.

I shake my head. "I design jewelry."

"Ohh." He watches me for a while very intently, and Mr. Minican floats into my mind, tapping his index finger on the confidentiality oath I had to sign to get the job. "As with any creative line, Amanda, we must expect a high degree of ... discretion ... from our employees." He'd have a coronary if he could see me now. But the whole thing's so ludicrous, so paranoid. The oath. The locked offices. The vault.

"I hope you're not a spy scooping designs from the spring line."

"Got me." He puts his hands up. "What are those anyway? They look like some sort of weird modern art."

"They're aboriginal, actually. Australian." I look at the ancient symbols I've drawn onto rings, pendants, bracelets.

"Where do you find them?" he asks.

The conductor announces my stop. I snap the sketchbook shut, slip it into my bag. "Sorry," I say, leaning toward him a little, "but that's top secret stuff." I slide my bag onto my shoulder. "And this is where I get off."

He stands to let me out. "My stop's Huntington," he says. "Nice talking to you."

"I enjoyed it."

"I'm Philip, by the way."

"Amanda."

The car stops, the doors open, I move away from him.

"Amanda?"

I turn around.

"You forgot something." He holds my umbrella out to me.

Nice, I think, moving with the flow of commuters heading across the platform for the stairs.

At the bottom step I glance up toward the exit to see if it's a drizzle or a downpour, but it's not either. For the first time in four days the gray is gone, the air's bright, the sky is almost blue.

"Is that sunshine?" someone beside me says. And then someone else, "Can you believe it?"

Looking up at the color of the sky, I feel my balance coming back, simple as that. A little sun, a little exchange on the train. I start humming "Dream a Little Dream of Me," and that's when I see him, just a glimpse through the spaces left by the commuters climbing the stairs. *Ramón.*

It's the last thing I'm expecting, to see Ramón of all people in the station at this hour of the morning, so I don't do any of the things I should—yell his name or aim my umbrella at his back. I just stand there on a step, staring as he rises into the sunlight, at that thick curly hair shaping his head, the smooth line of his suit across his shoulders. Then he reaches the top, turns the corner into the bright morning air, and poof, he's gone.

A girl with two rings in her nostril pushes by me. "This ain't no escalator, you know," she says.

Two seconds later I'm pushing past her. I weave my way around, squeeze through, shove when I have to. I step on somebody's foot. I slam shoulders with a guy in a sweatshirt. "Sorry," I say. "Sorry. Sorry," and keep going. Because the only thing on my mind right now is Ramón and how much I want to catch him. How much I want to grab him by his elegant elbow and ask him who the hell he thinks he is anyway. How much I want to let him know that I'm seriously pissed. Fucking angry. No shit.

At the top, I head in the direction he disappeared, half blind in the sudden light. "Goddamn sun," I mutter. I grope in my bag for my shades, but they aren't much help. Ahead of me there's a sea of heads charging across the intersection, heading down half a dozen sidewalks, and he may be distinctive, but he's not all that distinctive.

I start to drift in the other direction, looking back over my shoulder every few seconds, while it all sort of churns around inside me—fury, frustration, all the things I didn't get to say—until it starts to boil over and I say what the hell, and right there in the middle of the sidewalk, I stop, turn around, stick my arm up, and give him, wherever he is, the finger.

People pour around me. No one seems to notice. And then I see someone waving.

"Shit." I turn around and break into a trot, try to make myself small.

"Amanda! Wait!"

I jog a block, make it across the street after the Don't Walk goes solid, throw myself at the revolving doors of One Prospect and squeeze into Elevator A.

I catch a glimpse of Carter halfway across the lobby just as the elevator door slides shut. His face is red. His tie is crooked. Why in hell won't he just give up?

I clutch my bag to my chest and start feeling around inside for my office keys. That's when I discover that my sketch pad's gone.

CHAPTER TWO

Ramón broke a bread stick in half and scooped up some of the cheese spread. This was his favorite café. Off the beaten path. Tasteful. Private. The kind of place nobody would take a cockroach like Richie unless it was to win a bet. Or maybe settle a grudge. Or get some information.

The spread was garlicky, pungent, a pleasure to the tongue. He pushed the dish toward Richie. "Try this," he said.

Richie stuck his finger into the middle of it, then into his mouth. He smiled. "Tha's pretty good."

Ramón smiled back, dropped the rest of his bread stick onto his plate. "Now," he said, "you have something to tell me?"

Richie nodded. He drained his wineglass and wiped his hand across his mouth, then he leaned forward across the table, and Ramón had to fight against an urge to back away. "It's somethin' big," Richie said. "Somethin' very very big."

Ramón nodded. That, he'd already surmised. He picked up his wineglass and studied the pale pink liquid. He didn't want to seem anxious for Richie's information. You never wanted to let him think he might have the upper hand, just in case he was hiding a brain under that low forehead.

"Don't you wanna know?" Richie said.

"Oh yes, yes." He set the wineglass down. "I'm listening, Richie. Go ahead."

"It's so big that Manny said I had to leave before he took the call."

Ramón frowned. "Then you found out nothing?"

Richie slapped the table. "Shit man, what do you think I am? I just run upstairs and grabbed the walkie-talkie."

"The walkie-talkie." Ramón relaxed a little. "Very good, Richie." He and Manny had fought over that. Over Manny's cellular phone.

"It's not secure," Ramón had told him. "You might as well be writing whatever you're saying in the sky." "Ehh, you're a fucking paranoid" was Manny's answer. And so it served the sonofabitch right.

The dessert cart rolled up to the table, and the waiter stood there with a set of silver tongs poised above a chocolate-dusted napoleon. "May I interest either of you gentlemen in dessert?" he asked. There was the slightest hesitation before the word "gentlemen," and Ramón glanced up. The waiter had his eyes on Richie.

Richie leaned toward the cart. "What's that?" he said, pointing at a cream puff. The waiter explained. "How 'bout that?"

"A strawberry tart," the waiter answered.

"I dunno," Richie said, "they all look good." He touched the napoleon and then a rum baba.

"Sir!"

"He'll have them both," Ramón said quickly, wondering if he'd ever have the guts to come here again.

The waiter scooped the desserts onto a dish, set the dish on the edge of the table, and rattled the cart off toward the kitchen.

Richie popped the whole napoleon into his mouth. Like he was eating a goddamn Twinkie, for Christ's sake. The baba went next. He looked at his empty wineglass, then at the empty wine bottle.

"Take mine," Ramón said. He'd lost his appetite before the entrée arrived anyway.

Richie drained the glass. He grinned. An unfortunate grin, as though he didn't quite have equal control over both sides of his mouth. "It's two dogs fuckin'," he said. He giggled.

Ramón looked around to see if anyone had overheard. He looked back at Richie.

"The goods," Richie said. "What Manny has. It's two dogs fuckin'." He grinned again. "But these dogs got brains."

It took Ramón a second to put it together. "You mean, Manny has a legitimate find?"

Richie nodded. "Mexican." He giggled again. "Two dogs fuckin'."

"Colima dogs, Richie? Pre-Columbian?"

Richie shrugged. "Dunno."

"How in hell did he get it?"

Richie shrugged. "Dunno. But now he's gettin' the papers and he's happy as a suckin' pig. And that's what the call was all about. About pickin' up the papers."

Ramón took the napkin off his lap and placed it on the table. He'd asked Manny flat out, "You got something cooking, primo? A deal sweet enough to tell your cousin about?" Because there was something about Manny when he saw him the last time. Something. "Sweet?" Manny said. "Me? With things so bad I can hardly pay to keep little Manuel in the private school he needs? Nah. Nada. As dry as the desert, that's how things are." The lying bastard.

Ramón folded the napkin in half. "You want another dessert, Richie? More wine?"

Richie shook his head. He burped. "Nah. I'm stuffed. It was real good."

"I'm glad, Richie. I'm glad you enjoyed it." He laid his knife across the top of his spoon. Straightened them both into a perfect letter T. "So I suppose these papers have a price?"

"Fifty grand," Richie said. "Manny's meetin' the jockey at the usual place tomorrow at three."

Ramón's hand hit the tip of the knife and the T turned into a sideways V. He could feel his face getting red.

"So you want I should keep my ears open?" Richie said.

Ramón wasn't certain he could trust his voice. He nodded. "Sure," he said. "Sure." Richie looked at him. Ramón shifted his weight sideways and took his money clip out of his pocket. He peeled a five-hundred-dollar bill off the top. He started to put the clip away, but then he pulled off one more bill and slid them across the table to Richie.

"Jeez." Richie smelled the bills, then he stuck them in his pocket. "This is a hell of a lot."

"You did a good job, Richie," Ramón said. "You did a real good job."

It took him from the time he left the café until he hit the north side of the river to calm down enough to think. He pulled the Maserati into the right-hand lane and slid the window down all the way to let the cool air off the water clear his head. The fucking little asshole had hit the jackpot, and not the backdoor jackpot, a legitimate find, an authentic artifact with credentials. And, Jesus . . . if he was paying fifty grand, what did the fucker expect to clear at the end?

Why? Why in hell did the wind always blow at the guy's fucking fat back? It had nothing to do with smarts, that was certain. Which meant it was just dumbass luck. Some had bad. Some had good. Manny, his seemed always to come up good. Ramón passed a blonde driving a white '68 Corvette. She turned her head and met his eyes as he passed her. He smiled.

He'd been a gofer for Manny long enough to know how the fat sonofabitch operated, backward and forward. He knew his markup, his percentages. Manny was a conservative businessman. He applied the same arithmetic to a fifty-buck coin as he did to a five-thousand-dollar amphora. Cost times fifty, and costs never, never exceeded seven percent of the take. So if he was willing to pay fifty grand for the papers, and he'd already paid for the item . . . Ramón did the math in his head. Then he did it again. Jesus Christ. Even if he stole the fucking item, that was close to two million bucks.

He took the next exit and headed downtown. He needed a place to sit, a double scotch with another right behind it. He needed to think about this long and hard. But most of all, he needed to think about this smart. Very very smart.

He turned left at the second light and started looking for a place to park near his favorite bar. Manny had kept it to himself, the fucker. Not a whisper. "We're family, Ramón. You and me, primos, cousins, brothers under the skin. We look out for each other, right? Like our mothers would have wanted."

Like you looked out for me in Guatemala, *hermano*, huh? The sonofabitch. The thought of those years still made his stomach crawl, brought the taste of bile up in his mouth.

You see, Manny, *primo mio*, the jails of Guatemala have no bathrooms, no pillows, no electricity, no food that doesn't move. And the whole time I was in there, you know what the thing was that kept me from losing my fucking mind? It was the thought of you, Manuel. The hundred different ways I could kill you. The hundred different ways I could make you wish you'd done your duty by me instead of leaving me to suffer in hell for three years.

Ramón pulled over and waited for a car to pull out of a parking space. And Manny had no clue. No clue there was anything in his heart besides gratitude. Because that's what kind of a dumb sonofabitch Manny was. Since his own nervous system functioned like a worm's, only in response to immediate stimulation, he thought everyone's functioned that way. After three long years Ramón returned to an upscale shop, with the red Maserati parked out front and a bankbook slipped inside his pocket. Everything before that was forgotten. Or so

Manny thought. The betrayal, the lice, the filthy, stinking sleepless nights, the years lost from his life.

Inside the bar, Gerald nodded his bald head at him and lifted the good scotch from its place under the bar. "Make it a double," Ramón said.

When Gerald set it down on the table, Ramón handed him a twenty-dollar bill. "Keep them coming," he said.

He'd left Manny last Thursday knowing something wasn't right. Because when you were someone's shadow since before you could remember, you sensed that person like you sensed yourself. Manny had taught him to piss standing up. He'd loaned him Felicia so he could learn to fuck. They'd slept in the same room enough years so Ramón knew when Manny was going to fart. And now the bastard thought he could keep him on the outside on this.

Gerald set down the second scotch and picked up the empty glass as the door opened and three sailors walked in. They were loud, their walks, voices, gestures, everything about them, so that their presence charged the air in the bar, filled it with motion. But it didn't matter anymore. Ramón took a sip from the new drink, then he downed it and stood up. What he was going to do had been inside him, coiled like a snake all along, waiting for something to release it.

Manny looked surprised when Ramón walked into the office. Then he smiled. "Ramón," he said, "*Hermano*. What are you doing here?" He pushed himself out of his chair. The width of him seemed greater all the time. A soft, sour-smelling mountain of flesh. The two men embraced.

Ramón sat down and slid back against the leather sofa. He put his feet on top of the newspapers spread across the low table and smiled up at Manny. "What kind of a greeting is that—'What are you doing here?' "

Manny grinned. He looked like he didn't want Ramón to get comfortable, but when Ramón undid the buttons on his suit jacket and folded his arms, Manny sat down. "I have a busy day, Ramón. But I always have time for you." He glanced at his watch, then leaned forward. "Like I said, a busy day, with many things to do."

"While I, on the other hand, Manny, have nothing to do." Ramón smiled. "So why don't you let me do some of these things for you, huh? Or with you. Like the old days."

Manny shrugged. "Well, there are certain things a man can only do by himself, if you know what I mean?" He laughed, but it was a hollow, nervous laugh.

Ramón laughed along with him. "So it's those kinds of things you're doing. *Amor*."

Manny cleared his throat. He started gathering papers into a pile on his desk. "Those things and other things. But we'll get together later, Ramón. For dinner. When I have less on my mind." This time he looked directly at his watch and frowned. He stood up.

Ramón knew exactly what time it was. Two twenty-five. He knew that Manny always left fifteen minutes early for any meeting. He knew how long it took to get to St. Anthony's through midafternoon traffic. "Well then . . ." He lifted his feet off the table and set them on the floor, but didn't stand up. He slid forward on the leather seat. "How's Fernanda?"

"Fernanda is fine."

"She know about your plans this afternoon?" Ramón grinned.

Manny looked at him for a second, then he grinned, too. "Not those plans."

Ramón stood up. He bent down and picked up one of the newspapers, scanned some of the headlines. He could feel Manny's impatience like electricity in the air, and he was enjoying it.

Manny cleared his throat. "I'll call you, Ramón," he said. "We'll make plans for dinner."

Ramón dropped the paper back onto the table. "We'll talk soon," he said.

They embraced, and Ramón could feel the relief in Manny's hug. "*Adiós,* Manny," he said.

"*Adiós, primocito.*"

Ramón walked out onto the sidewalk. He slipped on his sunglasses as he passed the alley where Manny parked the Caddy. He'd ice-picked the rear passenger tire on his way in, and he figured it would take Manny maybe three blocks before he was riding the rim. Ramón got into the rented Ford and pulled out into traffic. This morning he'd talked Mickey into giving him ten days to redeem the Maserati. It wasn't all that much of a gamble. Because he'd get it back, and then buy two more. One to drive in the rain. One to drive on Sundays. Ramón smiled and headed for St. Anthony's.

The *mensajero*, the carrier, was waiting in the back pew at the far right of the deserted cathedral. Above him, the stained-glass window depicted the sad face of St. Teresa of the Roses, looking down at him as though he was one of her children. A window probably paid for with Manny's donations. A little insurance he provided himself just in case what he was doing in the back of the cathedral wasn't okay with God after all.

"I'm here for Manny's goods," Ramón said after he sat down. His voice disappeared into the air almost as soon as he'd spoken. He set his briefcase on the floor between his feet.

In the dim, colored light filtering through St. Teresa, there was something familiar about this *mensajero*, but Ramón couldn't come up with where or why.

"Manny said he was coming himself." The *mensajero* sat forward a little, tensed.

Ramón shrugged. "He sent me instead." Then he remembered. This was the Nicaraguan who'd carried goods into Belize for Manny before the Guatemalan fiasco. He dug hard into his memory for a fact, a name. "You remember me, amigo. Belize. The early eighties. Manny's cousin, Ramón. I picked up from you then, too." He hadn't, but he'd been there, so he remembered the circumstances, and it was long enough ago so this *mensajero* with bad breath probably didn't remember too many of the details. "On that fucking excuse for a road to the airport, amigo. In that heat. Even when the sun went down there was no relief."

The *mensajero* stood up. "I don't like last-minute changes. Tell it to Manny." He stepped into the aisle, and Ramón felt his stomach dropping out from under him. He tried to keep it out of his face, out of his voice. He shrugged. "So," he said, "then it will be two trips across town. And for the papers of two dogs fucking."

The *mensajero* stopped under a pool of rose-colored

light. He half turned, and Ramón couldn't be sure if
what he saw was a smile pulling at the corner of his lips
or a trick of the light.

"Belize," the *mensajero* said. He looked back at
Ramón.

Ramón forced himself to breathe. "With the storm
knocking out the power and no lights at the airport." He
shook his head as though he was remembering it almost
fondly.

"Manny's cousin," the *mensajero* said. "You have
something for me?"

Ramon tapped the briefcase.

The *mensajero* hesitated once more, then he sat down
again. "Still, I don't like last-minute changes."

"And Manny doesn't like it where he is either,"
Ramón said. "In the can with an attack of the shits."

The *mensajero* stifled a laugh.

Ramón relaxed a little, but he was beginning to feel
like he needed to get this over with and get the hell out
of there. Manny might end up driving all the way on the
rim for this one. "So," he said, pacing his words, keeping his body slack, "let's get this done before a bunch
of fucking nuns shows up."

The *mensajero* smiled.

Ramón reached for the briefcase and placed it between them on the pew. Then he unsnapped it. The
mensajero set the manila envelope he'd been holding
next to the briefcase.

The *mensajero* made a little sound when he saw the
money. He took a penlight out of his pocket and stuck
it into the briefcase, started picking up each banded
stack and riffling through them.

Inside the envelope Ramón found a stack of papers. Site photographs, grid drawings, descriptions, carbon dating reports. A letter of authentication from the government. Jesus Christ. It *was* pre-Columbian. From the Yucatán peninsula. Teotihuacán. The Temple of Quetzalcoatl. His hands started to shake. He put everything together and slid it back inside the folder at the same moment the *mensajero* snapped the briefcase shut.

"Tell Manny we'll do business again."

"I will," Ramón said.

It was over in ten minutes, that was what his watch said. For some reason, it felt much longer.

At the top of the marble steps he overcame the urge to run. He ended up having to walk up and down two streets before he found the Ford. He couldn't remember what it looked like, what color it was, where he'd parked it. His hands shook putting the key into the door, into the ignition. And then it hit him, sitting there, with people walking by, traffic in the street, a jet flying low overhead and drowning out everything else. He'd done it. He'd fucking done it.

Looking at the envelope on the seat beside him, he started to smile. Manny was going to suffer like hell. He was going to suffer almost as bad as if he were in a Guatemalan jail. And Ramón knew he was going to enjoy every fucking moment of it.

CHAPTER THREE

Charlene walks into my office while I'm sitting there dialing Ramón's number, and I almost hang up. I mean, we're back to normal, Charlene and I, but there's still this little hill of resentment I have to push myself over every once in a while, and I'm not all that certain I want her knowing every single intimate detail of my life anymore. Even if she did beg me to forgive her with tears in her eyes, and then go out and buy me that full-length wool sweater coat I'd been wanting for over two years. Although, when you think about it, that's probably the least someone you've known since the first day of kindergarten can do when she's gone out with your husband behind your back.

"You weren't even living together, Amanda," she said when I first found out, almost four years ago. "You'd already hired the lawyer and everything."

"Well, if it was so perfectly innocent and okay, then why didn't you tell me?" I asked her.

She didn't answer right away. "Because I knew it was a lousy thing to do," she said finally. Then her chin quivered. "But I'd been waiting for someone like Gary to ask me out my whole life."

After that, I couldn't have stayed mad even if I'd wanted to.

I hold up one finger, and she nods and sits down next to my drawing board. She starts looking through my sketches. "Oooooh," she says. She holds up the koala earrings. Charlene has this thing about Australia.

Ramón's phone rings its sixth ring and then the machine kicks in. "*Hola*. This is Ramón . . ."

It makes me furious all over again to have to sit there and listen to that message one more time. I jab my pencil into the drawing board, and the tip breaks off and flies into Charlene's hair. She looks at me as though I did it on purpose.

"Ramón," I say, "for the last time, these are the things I want back: my waffle iron, my Harry Chapin tape, my shower stuff, my purple tights, the Juarez pictures, and my grandmother's quilt. And I better hear from you by four-thirty this afternoon, that's Friday, the seventeenth, or else I—" The machine starts beeping at me and keeps beeping at me. I slam the phone down hard.

"You're dangerous today," Charlene says. Her eyes narrow. "You mean you actually gave him your grandmother's quilt?"

"I did not *give* him the quilt. I *brought* the quilt over there because he has this thing about turning the air conditioner up full-blast all night."

"That's because he's hot-blooded," she says. "All Latinos are hot-blooded."

"I don't care what he is," I tell her. "I just want my things back."

"It's his way of holding on to you." She picks up a

pencil and starts rolling it back and forth between her palms. "Having your things around, he can delude himself into thinking you're coming back."

Charlene listens to Dr. Brian Smith on the radio every afternoon from noon to three. She's developed this annoying habit of having an explanation for everything. Things you don't even want an explanation for. Like my habit of eating a peanut butter and fluff sandwich every day when I get home from work.

"It's because it represents a safe and secure time in your life," she says. "A time when things were simple and gratification was easy to come by."

"It's not possible I eat them just because I like the way they taste?"

"Oh no, Amanda. Nothing's as simple as all that."

She tosses the pencil into the air, tries to grab it, misses, then disappears after it under the drawing board.

"Anyway," I say, "I wouldn't call a person who's ignored all your phone messages for the last three months deluded. I'd just call him a jerk."

Her hand appears, holding up a wrinkled memo from accounting. "Speaking of delusion, is Carter still at it? He still thinks it's going to happen?"

"Don't remind me," I say. "I almost got hit by a taxi trying to avoid him this morning."

Her hand and the memo disappear. "It seems to me," she says from somewhere down around my knees, "that by now even a person like Carter should start to get suspicious about the whole idea." She pops up and drops the pencil on my board.

"He seemed so normal," I say, "so sane. Didn't he, Char? I mean, an accountant. Gray pinstriped suits. With vests, for Pete's sake. Am I crazy? Didn't he seem absolutely normal to you?"

"Oh yeah," she says, nodding her head. "Absolutely." She shrugs. "It's kind of sweet, though, you know? That he'd want you there with him when it happened. What does he call it, this thing he's waiting for?"

"Being raptured," I say.

"Right. Being raptured. Like he wants the two of you together for eternity." Then she stares at me for a second. "Guess he never got to know you very well, huh?"

I smile. I pick up a pack of gum and wave it at her. She shakes her head. "And then I went and left my sketchbook on the train this morning. With all my spring sketches." I slide out a stick, unwrap it, bite off a piece, and wrap up the other half again. "Which gave me a little over an hour to reinvent everything in the whole line, which I practically did. Until Mr. M called down at the last minute and canceled our meeting."

She groans. She's looking at the koala earring sketch again. Then she looks at a piece of paper next to it. She frowns. "What the heck is this?" She picks it up.

It's covered with shattered numbers. Ones and sevens that look like they're having nervous breakdowns, exploding, screaming, disintegrating.

"Doodles," I say.

"Doodles?" She shakes the paper. "From where? Hell?"

"Char." I grab for the paper. "It's nothing."

"Nothing?" she says, pulling it away and examining it.

"It's the date, Char. Today's."

"So?"

"And doodling is unconscious. It has nothing to do with anything meaningful."

She waves the paper a little.

"It's four years. Today."

She looks at me like she doesn't get it. Then she gets it. "Oh. That."

I take the paper, crumple it up, and toss it in the wastebasket.

"Bad morning, huh?"

I tap my eraser on the board. "No, not bad at all. I talked to someone on the train. Philip. Who gets off at Huntington."

"Nice?"

"Nice."

"Hmpf." She slumps back against the chair. "Nothing like that would happen to me in a million years."

It's the kind of thing she says all the time. It drives me crazy. Because there she is—big brown eyes, a great smile, a sense of humor—and all she can focus on is her nose. As if that's all Charlene Marie Campanelli is. A nose.

"Char . . ."

"I know, I know. Bad attitude." She stands up. "So let's make a deal, you and me. You quit moping over your little anniversary, and I'll quit moping over my little lack of self-esteem."

"Char, I am not moping. I thought about it for five minutes this morning. Five minutes."

"And I am not being negative," she says. "I am being realistic. Realistic." We eye each other for about three seconds. "Anyway, I have to get back to work." She stops in the doorway and turns around. "If you want, come on over tonight. We're doing legs."

Charlene's a Rolfer. She believes that every trauma you have gets stored in your muscles. On Fridays a bunch of them get together and practice deep massage.

"Okay. Maybe I will."

"It'll be late, so if you come, plan to stay over. Maybe we can locate where your divorce is and get rid of it once and for all."

I toss my eraser at her, but she closes the door behind her fast, and it whacks the wood. Then I wait for her to open it again, because she knows I can't stand it in here with the door shut, but she doesn't.

After a while I get up and open it myself. Not that I mind that my office used to be a closet. After all, it's more than I ever thought I'd have. Although, when I think about it, I wasn't actually unhappy being Mr. Minican's secretary. And if I hadn't walked in on his meeting, I'd probably still be up there typing his letters and taking dictation.

"It's not right," he was saying when I opened the door. "No one's going to want a monkey pendant that looks like it's going to bite you in the neck."

I could have waited to give him his mail. But after hearing that, I was curious. I wanted to see that monkey. So I glanced down over his shoulder when I set the mail on his desk, and he was right. The monkey looked like it needed to be shot.

Then he held the photograph up and sort of half turned toward me. "What do you think, Amanda? How would you feel if somebody gave you this?"

All they were expecting was a simple "I'd love it," or

"I'd hate it." But I've been drawing since I was old enough to hold a crayon, and this monkey had some pretty basic problems.

"Frankly," I said, "I wouldn't be very pleased."

"You see?" he said, turning back to the others.

"The biggest problem is in the eyes," I continued. "They're too small and they're too close together. And the distance between the nose and mouth is too big and too flat. You know, like Richard Nixon."

They looked at me. It got very quiet.

"Like this," I said. I picked up a pencil and sketched a monkey that looked more like the pope, kind and loving. Then I sketched one that looked innocent and another that looked wistful. "Personally," I said, putting down the pencil, "I'd go with wistful. It'll make people want to rescue it."

So now I have my own office, my own drawing board. I even have my own tiny window. I watch the traffic rolling along silently below, and I wish it were as easy to rearrange things in real life as in a sketch. A line here, a shadow there. Then maybe I could rescue Mama. Draw her mind all seamless and sharp again.

"You tell that husband of yours to quit honking his horn out front every night, Amanda."

It's something we go through every time we talk.

"That's not Gary, Mama. That's someone else honking out front. And Gary is not my husband anymore, remember?"

"And to think, your cousin Suzanne, who's not half as pretty as you or half as smart, and she goes and marries a man who has degrees! And you, you end up with Evel Knievel."

Not that hating Gary came with the Alzheimer's. Hating Gary may be one of the only things she *does* remember. Before the wedding, I used to have night frights that he wouldn't show up. Why should he, I kept telling myself, when everybody on one side of the aisle was going to be sitting there hoping his bike would ram a bridge abutment on the way to the ceremony.

The phone rings.

"It occurred to me," Charlene says, "that the last thing I heard you say to Ramón's answering machine was 'or else.' Or else what?"

"Or else nothing," I say. "Or else, period. Why? What did you think it meant?"

I can hear her pushing buttons. She takes care of fifteen lawyers on the twenty-second floor, and she probably has thirty people on hold right now. "I don't know," she says. "I just wanted to check."

" 'Bye, Char," I say. "It'll be fine."

"Yeah, well. 'Bye."

Twenty-three years ago I cracked the kid next door on the back of the legs with his own baseball bat because he wouldn't stop hitting his dog. To this day, Charlene thinks I have the potential to be dangerous.

I sharpen my pencil, start working on a kangaroo pendant. Every once in a while I glance at the telephone, then at the clock. Three comes and goes, three-thirty, four. He doesn't call. My kangaroos go downhill with the minute hand, from sweet to sour to downright mean. The last one I draw is wearing boxing gloves and snarling.

I give him ten extra minutes, fifteen. Then I line up my pencils and erasers on the drawing board, gather my sketches, and lock them in the vault. I rummage through my shoulder bag and take out my key ring, holding it up by a small greenish key. The key to Ramón's apartment.

"Okay, Ramón," I say. "Here I come, ready or not."

CHAPTER FOUR

If it hadn't been for the Russian dolls, I never would have met Ramón. They're the only reason I walked into his antique shop in the first place. I have this thing about them, about the way they nest inside each other, so that opening them is one nice surprise after another. There were two in the window. A set of pigs and an unusual set of crocodiles, and on an impulse, I went inside.

The pigs were cheaper, but the crocodiles were something I'd never seen before, and I almost decided to splurge on the crocs but realized I should go back to the pigs.

"Theeese are the better buy." He tapped the crocodiles. "Because they are unique, one day their value will be higher."

"Well, it's their value today that's the problem," I said, looking at him, and the first thing I remember thinking was how I liked the way his hair curled against the edge of his collar. That was something I was vulnerable to just then, right after Carter, whose hair and collar were separated by a good inch and a half of very clean white neck.

27

I looked at the crocs again. "I'm afraid they'd stretch my budget a bit too much right now."

"Ahh." Ramón nodded as though I'd told him something very important. He had that way about him, of taking every little thing you said in a very serious way. And then he smiled. A smile that could melt ice.

"Well then," he said, "the pigs, they are very nice, too."

He told me he was an importer/exporter. I'd never met an importer/exporter. He left me alone until I decided, finally, on the pigs, and then he walked me to the door. I remember thunder rumbling very near and a strange green-gold light to the air. Dust was blowing along the sidewalk, and then it began to rain. "Ahh," he said, "no one will come to the shop in this weather." He pointed across the street to a café. "We could wait out the storm in there, no? Ramón and . . . ?"

"Amanda."

"Amaahnda."

No one had ever said my name quite that way before.

What we had was nice—for a while. A little like getting on a roller coaster at the amusement park—going up and down, getting a nice view at the top, and this sensation that takes your breath away. And if you try, you can almost fool yourself into thinking you're actually going somewhere, except that when the ride's over, there you are in the same exact spot you were in when you got on. Not that I hold that against Ramón. It's not his fault we were looking for different things. But what I do hold against him is the last four months. I mean, how many times do you have to ask someone to do one simple thing? "Drop the stuff on my lawn, Ramón, or mail it to me. Toss it all on your sidewalk and I'll come over and pick it up!" And he kept promising . . . "Amaahnda, oh noooo, I forgot again. What eees wrong with me? I have been sooo busy. But I will drop it off. Tomorrow. No, tonight. I will do it tonight."

I pull into a space across from his town house, turn the key, and scan the cars parked up and down the street. No red Maserati. Not that it matters, because whether he's home or not, I'm getting my things.

I lock the car, cross the street, step up on the sidewalk, and wait for a woman with twins to push her carriage by. I smile at the two identical little faces and then at her. She smiles back, but she has these huge circles under her eyes. She looks as though she hasn't had a decent night's sleep in weeks. And seeing her tired look takes the edge off this little desire that pops up inside me like one of those Butterball turkey timers whenever I see something wrapped in a baby blanket.

I climb the brick steps to Ramón's door and knock. I ring the bell, knock again, ring the bell one more time. Then I use the key, and when the door opens, there's that familiar smell—a sort of musky, musty odor of old things packed away for a long time.

"Ramón?" The sound of my voice evaporates into the silent rooms, and it occurs to me that the decision to come here may have been a trifle hasty. That if he walks in and finds me, he might not be exactly charmed. But then it also occurs to me that I'm not exactly charmed by him right now, either.

I step inside and close the door, but not all the way, because it's a tricky lock and I never did get the hang of it. And getting this over with and getting out fast

seems like a good idea. I walk soundlessly across the
thick carpet, through the front hall into the living room.
"Ramón?"

I'm setting my purse on a chair, when there's a noise
behind me, a click like a lock being thrown, that freezes
me right in the center of the white Oriental, and for a
couple of seconds all the blood in my body seems to
sink down toward the floor, until I hear the noise again
and, this time, recognize it. I turn around, feeling foolish, and look at the antique grandfather clock near the
stairs. He told me it took him two years to rebuild. His
pride and joy.

The gears whir, it clicks one more time, and strikes
the quarter hour. One, two, three. "Listen," he'd say,
whenever it struck midnight, "the sound of eternity calling, no?"

The sound dies away slowly, until, once again, it's
very very quiet.

On my way into the kitchen I pass his answering machine. It's blinking full, which explains why it cut me
off in the middle of my message.

In the kitchen, I open and close cupboards until I find
my waffle iron. I carry it back out to the front hall and
set it down on the floor. Through the window I catch a
glimpse of a red car going by, slowing, as though it's
looking for a place to park, and I freeze. But it's not
Ramón's car.

I start up the circular stairs, remembering how I felt
the first night he led me to his bedroom. A man with
eyes the color of Godiva chocolate. An importer/
exporter. A man who called me *Amaahnda*.

In the bedroom, I spot my grandmother's quilt and

my purple tights at the end of the bed as though they belong there. In the bathroom, I make a knot about knee high in the tights and drop my shampoo down one leg, my conditioner down the other. I open drawers, looking for the Juarez pictures, but all I find is that most of the drawers are empty. I check the closet. Mostly empty, too. Which means that he doesn't plan to be back for a while. I relax a little. I check the drawers one more time. I don't want to leave without those pictures.

Those damn pictures. I should never have listened to him. The thing that gets me is I'm old enough to know better. Sixteen-year-olds pose for those kinds of pictures. Though after half a bottle of tequila, I probably had no idea how old I was. I should have gone ahead and ripped them into a million pieces the day he picked them up. "But Amahnda, they are so beautiful." I slam the last drawer shut.

I check the bedroom stereo for my Harry Chapin tape. Not there. I go back downstairs and find it in the tape deck in the living room, half wound, as though it was the last thing he was listening to.

With the drapes drawn it's dark now inside, but I don't want to put on the lights. I go through the drawers in his desk by feel mostly, but the photos aren't there, either. And then the damned grandfather clock does it again, whirs, clicks, and even though I know what it is, it sets me all jumpy. "Damn him," I mutter, "what did he do with them, anyway?"

I rip a piece of paper off a pad. *Dear Ramón,* I write, *I decided to come over and get my things since your promises to return them were beginning to seem less*

than sincere. Here's your key. Juarez pictures? I under-
line the last two words twice and add three more question marks. I slide his key off my ring, put it on top of
the note.

That's when I notice the nesting dolls, the crocodiles,
sitting all by themselves on the bookshelf. Ramón gave
them to me on our second date, and we set them together on the shelf, the pigs and the crocs. A silly, sentimental thing to do. But I'm not feeling silly and
sentimental anymore. The pigs I bought aren't there, but
the crocodiles are, staring straight at me.

Then the phone starts to ring, and I jump. I grab the
crocs, drop them inside my tights, pick up the rest of
my things. As I pull the door closed behind me, the
phone's still ringing. As though it's never going to stop.

Outside, the sky is violet and the shadows of the
buildings stretch into the street. Lights are beginning to
go on in some of the windows, and as I dump everything into the trunk, I look up at Ramón's windows, all
dark, and for some reason, looking at them, I shiver.

CHAPTER FIVE

"Mama," I say, switching the phone from one hand to the other, "I can't do anything about your ants. What you have to do is tell the custodian about them. Mr. Jim, remember? With the red hair? You tell him about the ants and he'll take care of them." I throw a sweatshirt into the top of my plaid overnighter and hold the phone between my chin and my shoulder while I zip it shut.

"They're all over the place," she says. "Even the cat ran away."

"Mama, you don't have a cat. Now listen to me, okay? I'm not coming by tonight. I'm visiting Charlene. So if you need anything, it's Miss Jane who's going to be checking on you. You tell her if you need anything, okay?"

"Fuck," she says.

It doesn't matter how many times I hear it, I can't get used to it. Words I would have thought she didn't even know come out of her mouth just like they always belonged there.

"Fucking little bastards."

The doctor says to ignore it. That it's part of her

33

malady, as he calls it, and there's nothing anyone can do about it. But then, it's not *his* mother telling some stranger in the supermarket to get the fuck out of her way.

I hear water running. "What are you doing, Mama?"

"I just got the little sonsabitches," she says. "Three of 'em right down the fucking drain."

"Okay, good. Now, Mama, are you listening? I'm going to hang up, okay? I have to leave now. You tell Miss Jane if you need anything. Mama?"

"And you tell that husband of yours to quit riding that motorcycle outside my house every night. I need my sleep, you know."

"I know, Mama. You go lie down now, okay? Night-night."

I hang up the phone gently, as if somehow I'm hanging it up on her, really *on* her, and it hits me the way it always does that I should be there killing her ants and reminding her to pick up her sandwich and eat it. That I should be the one to tell her she forgot to button her blouse and that her friend, Missie, is not a selfish bastard, that the reason she hasn't called all day is because she died in 1974. It should be me doing those things instead of a bunch of strangers, because if it were reversed, and it were me losing my mind little by little, day by day, I know that all the armies in the world couldn't keep my mother away. But the thing is, I'm not there. I'm here, getting ready for a deep massage. And the truth is, I couldn't do it anyway. I'm just not that good.

Ringo lets out a whimper, and I look over at him. He blinks the eye with the black ring around it and starts a little dance near the door. He's having a hard time containing himself. He's been like this for an hour now, ever since I opened the gate and he came bursting out of the backyard. That's unusual for Ringo, bursting out of the backyard. Usually he takes his sweet time while I'm standing there holding the gate, especially if I'm standing there holding the gate in the rain. He sticks his nose out of his doghouse, then his head, then his shoulders, then he stretches and shakes himself a few times, and when he's good and ready, the rest of him comes out, and he does a slow trot over to the gate. But tonight was different. Tonight he was waiting at the gate making little noises, and he's been following me around ever since, acting impatient. As though somehow he knows we're headed somewhere. Knew it before I even got home.

Ringo's one of the two things I got the day we signed the divorce papers. Not that I asked for either one. Gary handed Ringo over right there on the courthouse steps. "Here." He handed me the leash. "He's yours, too."

"Gary," I said, "in case you've forgotten, you had Ringo before we got married. He's yours."

He shook his head. "Nope. He'll be better off with you. You're the one who feeds him. You're the one who remembers to take him to the vet."

"But you're the one he loves. You're the one he jumps all over at the end of the day. He hardly wags his tail at me."

"Well, maybe it's about time he learned the difference between who he can count on and who he can't." It was the first time I'd seen him look as though he was finally taking the whole thing seriously. Trouble was, by then it was way too late.

Then he turned around and walked out, and even though my lawyer grabbed on, too, we still got pulled halfway down the hall before Ringo gave up and just sat there and howled.

I grab my bag and check to make sure the hall and kitchen lights are on. "C'mon, Ringo," I say, "let's go." He lets out a squeal.

I head toward the highway, stick my Harry Chapin tape in. He starts singing, ". . . and I went off to find the sky." Exactly where Ramón must have stopped it. I hum along for a while, feeling good. I have my things back—well, almost all my things. I can finally start to nail the lid down on Ramón. And I have a whole weekend ahead of me to do whatever I want. I turn the volume up and slide into the middle lane, pull in behind a bottled-water truck that has a picture of a purple mountain and a green valley painted on its rear doors. I get closer, and my headlights pick out a lake and a little boat sitting in the middle of it. It makes me think of the cabin, the other thing I didn't want from Gary but got anyway.

I think about Charlene and her Rolfers. And I start to remember the last time I went, and how I kept insisting the massage hurt and how they kept insisting it didn't.

I check out the back of the truck one more time. "Hey, Ring, how about if we can Rolfing and head for the lake instead?"

He sits up in the backseat and cocks his head at me in the rearview mirror. I'd swear he nods.

I take the next exit, which deposits me in front of a

market where I can pick up the things I'll need for the weekend. Milk, cereal, juice, bread, dog food. I pull into the parking lot. "You stay here," I say to Ringo. "I'll be right back."

You can smell the change in the air when you get near enough to the lake, and you can feel it, too. The road to the cabin is dark and curvy and narrow, but I've driven it so many times, and there's hardly ever another car coming in the other direction.

I called Charlene from the market, just to let her know I wasn't coming.

"You're going up to that godforsaken place all by yourself?" she said.

"Want to join me tomorrow?"

"No thanks. But as soon as I get a yen for snakes and mice and mosquitoes, I'll let you know."

I turn into the driveway, shut off the lights, and sit there waiting for my eyes to get used to the dark. Ringo starts running across the backseat from one window to the other like he's crazy. "Will you stop?" I say.

Pretty soon I can see the shapes of the pine trees all around the cabin, then the shiny metal roof that makes music when it rains, and the outline of the porch Gary built, and the swing he bought me for my thirtieth birthday.

"Okay," I tell Ringo, "now that I can see, we can proceed."

I open my door and he jumps the front seat and runs right over me. I hear him rustling in the bushes on the edge of the pines. The last time we did this, he found a skunk in those bushes, and I ended up pouring tomato juice over him until three o'clock in the morning.

"Ringo! Get over here!" I grab my plaid bag and the groceries with one hand, and the keys and my half-dead flashlight with the other. The flagstones leading to the porch are partly covered with overgrown grass, and the bittersweet has grown all the way up the downspout onto the porch roof. Which means I'm going to have to wrestle with that damn lawn mower tomorrow and look for the clippers or else end up hacking at the vine with a pair of scissors the way I did last time. And it was my idea, too, the bittersweet. Because I liked the orange-red berries in the fall.

"You're going to plant that weed next to the porch?" That was Gary.

"This happens to be a decorative vine." That was me. And I've been trying to get rid of the damn thing for three summers now.

Ringo races up the stairs ahead of me to the door and stands there, panting, his front feet on the threshold as though getting inside is a life and death situation. I set the bags down so I can hold the flashlight while I work the key, but the flashlight has faded to almost nothing.

Ringo whines.

"Shhh. I'm doing this as fast as I can."

He scratches at the wood. Then the key finds the hole, and the door swings open.

He races in, his nails clicking across the pine floor.

I step in after him and start feeling with my free hand along the wall for the light switch, breathing in the familiar smell of pine and old wood fires and something else I can't quite get right away. Then it registers. Kentucky fried chicken.

My hand freezes on the wall just as Ringo growls, a throaty, mean warning sound that I've only heard come out of him at the vet. Then the hinges on the bedroom door start a low, slow squeal. Somebody yells "Don't move," and without even thinking, I heave the flashlight hard in the direction of the yell. Ringo starts barking, sounding more like a bear than a dog, and I hear a thunk, a "Goddammit," and then the sound of Ringo's barking flying through the air. Somebody screams, maybe me, then there's a crash, and that's when I turn and run.

CHAPTER SIX

"Ringo, goddammit Ringo, get off me!" That's what I hear as I'm running toward the car. Then Ringo stops barking and starts yelping, and even though I haven't heard him do that in a long time now, I still know exactly what it means. So I stop. I turn around. My fear begins to turn into something else.

The lights go on inside the cabin just as I get back to the door, and we all stand there blinking at each other. Me. Gary. And some girl wearing my Pink Panther tank top and nothing else.

"Ooooh," the girl says. She goes to step behind Gary, but as soon as she moves, Ringo stops wiggling and lowers his head. His top lip comes up, showing fangs I never even knew he had, and a sound comes out of him that makes even me go very still.

The girl freezes.

"Back off, Ringo," Gary says.

Ringo goes through this funny lightning quick change. He looks at Gary and his lip lowers, his head comes up, his tail gives one wag, and then he switches his attention back to her, and in an instant he's Ringo, wild dog of Borneo, again.

"Mandy, call him off, okay?" Gary says.

I look at Gary, trying to get it straight that it's really him standing there in a pair of plaid boxer shorts that match my overnight bag, standing there next to some girl who looks like Goldie Hawn with red hair, and that I'm not having an hallucination, that I'm not just reliving some really awful part of our past.

"Mandy, call him off."

The wheels in my brain start turning again. "I never called him *on*. Gary, what in hell are you doing here?"

He bends down and picks up my flashlight. Then he rubs the side of his head. "How did you manage that in the dark?" he says. He takes a step toward me. The girl puts a hand out after him, and once again Ringo growls and she goes back into instant freeze.

"It's kind of a long story," he says.

"Well, I can't wait to hear it."

He clears his throat. "We were out for a drive, Jennifer and I, and I got this urge to take a ride by the place. You know, show off the place I built." He smiles.

I don't smile back.

"And then we had a little problem with the car."

"Gaaarrry." Jennifer's lips barely move.

Ringo takes a step toward her, then another, until those fangs are about six inches from her thigh.

"He won't hurt you, Jen," Gary says. "He's all bluff."

"Oh really?" I say. "Like the time he bluffed eleven stitches into the vet's forearm?"

He seems to consider this for a second. Then he shakes his head. "Nah, he has this thing about vets, that's all. Trust me, Jen, he won't hurt you."

The words are barely out of his mouth when Ringo lunges at her. She screams, and Gary manages to grab onto his collar just long enough for her to get into the bedroom and slam the door.

"When did you teach him to do that?" Gary asks.

"I haven't taught him to do anything. He thought that one up all by himself."

Gary stares at me for a second, and then his look softens. "Hey, Mandy. How are you?"

"I asked you what you were doing here, Gary, and I haven't heard an answer yet."

"The car," he says. "It blew a water hose about a hundred yards up the road. So I had to get Joe to come out and tow it to the station. I figured you wouldn't mind if we stayed overnight. Especially since you weren't even here."

"I mind," I say.

All traces of the soft look disappear. "Right." He glances down at Ringo, who's staring up at him with this dumb happy look on his face. "Well, the thing is, the car won't be fixed until tomorrow morning."

"Well, the thing is, I don't care."

His eyes slide off me and he looks around the room. "I like what you've done to the place." He walks over to the new table, Ringo at his heels. He taps the top with his knuckles. "Nice," he says.

"I can't believe you still do that," I say.

"Do what?"

"Change the subject. Just because you don't like the one we happen to be on."

He crosses his arms. "Okay, Mandy. Back to your subject then." He nods his head toward me. "You first."

"Did you keep a key to the place just on the chance that your car might happen to break down out front some day?"

"No." He shakes his head. "Actually, I didn't. But the one over the door was there just like it always used to be."

"I want you out of here," I say.

"We will be. First thing in the morning."

"Now."

He stares at me for a good ten seconds. "What do you expect me to do, Mandy?" He says this in a whisper, as though the person in the bedroom might not already have a clue about what's going on out here. "Ask her to sleep under a tree?"

"Frankly, I don't care where she sleeps." I don't whisper. I say it loud enough to guarantee penetration through all the walls. "As long as it's not in my bed. And not in my clothes."

He looks around the room, as though maybe there'll be an answer to his predicament written on the walls or over the fireplace. "I'll be happy to leave," he says, "but I'd appreciate it if you'd at least let her stay the night. She didn't ask to come here. Or for this to happen."

"This is *my* house, Gary."

"I know that," he says. Then his voice goes low again. "I'm just asking you to do me a favor. For Pete's sake, Mandy, it's not like we're married anymore. I can go out with a woman and not have to worry about you getting all pissed off about it."

Now it's my turn to stare at him. "You mean you actually used to worry?"

He sighs. And that sigh takes me back to every fight we ever had. Me on one side of the room and him on the other. Though it might as well have been me on one side of the moon and him on the other, considering how precious little got through in the way of communication.

And here I am, I realize, taking up that same position on the moon out of pure habit. As if the last four years hadn't happened and we were just picking up where we left off the day I moved out. And is that, I ask myself, what you want? To let him think it still matters? That *he* still matters?

I take a deep breath. I let it out. "All right, of course you can stay. You can both stay. It was just . . ." I strike around for the right words. "It was just a little overwhelming, walking into it like this."

"Thanks," he says. "Thanks, Mand."

"Well, it's been a long day, and I'm tired and I'm going to bed. I'll sleep in the spare room." I pick up my bag that matches his shorts. "C'mon, Ringo."

At the door to the spare room, I stop and turn around. Ringo's standing about halfway between the two of us. He looks at Gary, then he looks at me, then he looks at Gary again. Neither one of us says a word. It takes him about twenty seconds to decide, and then he comes toward me, slowly. But he comes. And if he hadn't, I don't know what I would have done.

When I get into bed, I can hear them in the other room. At first their voices are low, then they get loud, and the fight lasts for about ten minutes. Then the bedroom door opens, closes, and the springs on the couch make a few noises. It gets quiet, very very quiet, and with him out there on the couch, a sort of old normal feeling settles over me that I can't make go away. I lie there in the dim moonlight coming through the curtain, looking up at the design of knots in the wood ceiling, listening to the wash of the lake against the shore, and wonder just what it is I gave him that I can't quite seem to get back.

I toss and turn for a while, and finally I fall asleep. I dream about Russian dolls, all painted to look like women, a brunette, a blonde, a redhead wearing my Pink Panther tank top. And when I open the very last one, the little doll inside is wearing plaid boxer shorts and looks just like Gary.

The smell of eggs and bacon trickles into my dreams, wakes me up, and for a few seconds I have no idea where I am. Then I remember. I look at my watch. Nine o'clock, and they're still here? It's like a shot of adrenaline. It gets me out of bed, washed, into my clothes, and keeps me mumbling to myself the whole time.

" 'Morning," Gary says when I walk into the kitchen. He's standing at the stove with a spatula in one hand and a plate in the other. Ringo's sitting right up next to his leg. "Ringo wanted out about an hour ago," he says. "You were sound asleep. Breakfast?"

I look toward the other bedroom, through the open door, where my tank top is laid out on top of the quilt, then back at him.

"Gone," he says. "Before I woke up. She was a little upset."

"What do you mean gone? Gone where?"

"Walked up to the garage. Joe said she was already

there waiting for the car when he opened up. He
dropped off the bill a little while ago."

"She took your car?"

He nods.

"But she's coming back to get you, right?"

He shrugs. "That wasn't part of the message."

"Wasn't part of what message?"

"The one Joe delivered along with the bill."

I wait. He flips three eggs in the pan, one, two, three,
and it reminds me how I could never do that. He shrugs.
"Like I said, she was upset."

He slides an egg out of the pan onto a dish, adds
some bacon, two pieces of toast. He holds the dish out
to me and I take it, because there doesn't seem to be
anything else to do.

He carries his plate over to the table and sits down.
"C'mon, Mandy," he says, "it'll get cold."

I sit down across from him. It feels strange and not
strange at the same time.

"So what are you going to do?" I ask.

He breaks off a piece of bacon and gives it to Ringo.
"Well, right now, I'm going to eat breakfast, and then I
think I'm going to take Ringo for a walk. Maybe by the
time I get back, Joe'll have scared up a rental for me.
He said it might take a while."

I nod. It all sounds vaguely reasonable.

"How's your mother?" he asks.

"Fine," I say. "Healthy. She just has trouble remembering whether it's her socks or her shoes that go on
first." I take a bite of my bacon. "She talks about you
often."

"I bet she does. She yelled at me for a good five min-

utes the last time I went to see her. She says I keep her
up all night long. Riding my bike up and down the
street in front of her place." He looks at me and grins.
"Though I think what she said was 'all fucking night
long.'"

"You went to see her?"

"Yeah. Isn't that okay?"

"Well . . . sure, it's okay. I just didn't know."

He scoops out some jelly and layers it across a piece
of toast. "She never liked me," he says. "I mean, that
was no secret. But she had this way about her, you
know? She met you square on. Never threw a punch
when you weren't looking. And I liked that about her.
Anyway, she doesn't seem to mind if I drop by once in
a while." He shakes his head. "She sure can swear,
though." He starts in on his second egg.

There's something about the way he says it: *She sure
can swear, though.* As if he's offended by it. Gary, of all
people, offended by my mother's cursing. The whole
idea of it is funny. And the more I try not to let it be
funny, the funnier it gets. I cover my mouth with my
hand. Gary looks up. He smiles. I try not to laugh. He
picks up a piece of bacon and looks at it. I bite my lip.
"Really," he says, "worse than any biker I ever met."
Which starts both of us off, except that after a few
minutes I'm not laughing anymore, I'm crying. And I
don't seem to be able to stop. I push myself up from the
table and head for the porch. I wrap my arms around a
post when I get there and wonder what in hell is wrong
with me.

"Mandy," Gary says. He puts his hands on my shoulders. "Jeez, Mandy."

"She's going away," I say. "I'm losing her."

"I know," he says. "I know."

We stand there, me hugging the post, him hugging me and the post until whatever it is is all out, all gone.

"I'm okay," I say, wiping my nose on my sleeve. "I don't know why I did that."

"I do," he says. "Something terrible is happening to someone you love right in front of your eyes, while you stand there and watch, and there's not a goddamn thing you can do to stop it."

He goes into the house, and when he comes back, he's carrying a box of tissues. "Here," he says. He crosses over to the other side of the porch and stands there looking out at the lake. "I thought I'd take Ringo and make the loop around the lake," he says, "and what I'm thinking is that he'd like it better if you came along."

I blow my nose one last time, shake my head. "I don't think so. You go ahead."

"C'mon, Mandy," he says. "It's just a walk."

Ringo hears the word and starts bouncing all over the porch. He jumps on me, then he jumps on Gary, then he jumps on me again.

"Okay," Gary says. "Now go ahead and tell him after all that you're not going."

As though they rehearsed it, Ringo nudges my hand with his nose, then he sits down and puts one paw on my leg.

"Okay, okay. But give me a few minutes."

"I'll clear the stuff off the table," Gary says.

In the bathroom, I look at myself in the mirror. My eyes and my lips are puffy. My nose is red. I splash

cold water on my face and tell myself that it's perfectly
sensible to think that Gary and I should be able to
spend a couple of hours together without all the bad
stuff getting in the way.

I pick up my hairbrush. It has red hairs in it. I pick
them out and drop them in the wastebasket. Then I run
the brush through my hair and set it back down on the
sink. You can do this, I tell myself. You can do this.

CHAPTER SEVEN

Ramón smiled and hit the four digits that told his answering machine at home to rewind. Manny wanted to kill him. He could hear it in his voice. Amanda didn't sound happy either. But he guessed that between the two of them, he would have more trouble with Manny.

The shit had been in the fan for almost twenty-four hours. Long enough to let Manny suffer with not knowing. Now it was time to let him suffer with knowing.

It felt good, the whole thing resting in the palm of his hand like a very big, very cool, very high-priced marble.

He rearranged the pillows under his head, picked up the receiver again, and punched in Manny's number. The marbles had always belonged to Manny. When they were kids playing in the street, because he was older. When they were punks trying to get out of the barrio, because he was meaner. When they started moving goods, because he was more careful. And always, he had been a little luckier.

Until now.

Ramón looked at the beige motel drapes, the beige motel prints on the wall, the beige motel hangers

welded into the beige motel rod, the beige motel TV
bolted down on the beige motel furniture. He was in
such a good mood that none of it even bothered him.
Because soon, very soon, he'd have everything. He
thought about his grandfather clock. He'd never let it
run down before and it made him feel bad. But
Manny'd have someone outside the house, because
Manny was pissed. He'd have someone outside the
shop, outside the restaurant where Ramón ate on Saturday nights, outside the salon where he had his hair done
every two weeks, outside Carla's apartment. He might
even have someone outside the place where he'd had
breakfast once in 1992. That's how pissed Manny was.
Mucho inflamado. He smiled when he heard his cousin's voice.

"Yeah?"

"Is that any way to answer the phone?" Ramón said.

"You sonofabitch! When I get my hands on you I'm
going to rip out your heart!"

"Calm down, Manny," he said, "because if you keep
yelling, you're going to miss all the important information I'm about to give you."

"You think this is a joke, you little *bastardo*. But
what you're playing with isn't funny. And it isn't smart.
And it isn't going to give you a long life, *niño*."

Ignoring the threat, Ramón said, "There are two
things I need to communicate to you. One, you already
know. That I have the goods. Bought and paid for. The
other thing is that it will cost you half a million to get
it back."

There was a scream on the other end of the phone,
like a pig being stuck with a knife, then the sound of

something smashing. After a while, Manny's voice, very quiet now, very low.

"I will give you nothing," he said. "You will come to me and you will tell me where the goods are, and for the sake of our mothers, for our *sangre*, our blood, I will forget this thing ever happened."

Ramón bolted off the bed. His intention had been to stay calm, to let Manny be the one to rant and rave. But he could feel the pounding in his own temples now. "And where was our blood, Manuel, in Guatemala? Where was our blood for the three years you lived like a *patrón* and I lived like a *sabandija*, a vermin?"

There was silence on the other end of the line. Manny cleared his throat. "Go to hell, you bastard," he said. "And I'll go there myself before I'll pay you this blood money."

Ramón relaxed his grip on the phone. This was going to go his way only by staying in control. By working Manny the way you worked any beast of low intelligence and high cunning. "Blood money!" he said. "C'mon, Manny. Either we both win or we both lose. It's not such a hard decision. Think of it as an easing of your poor conscience." He counted to five. "I'll give you twenty-four hours to reconsider, and then I'll burn the goddamn thing." He hung up, dropped the phone on the bed, and reached for the doorknob. In the next room, Carla was sitting on the beige motel couch with a magazine opened on her bare cinnamon-colored legs. She looked at him, and then slid the magazine sideways onto the couch and got up. He watched her walking toward him. She'd never lose that walk. They'd live in Beverly Hills, surrounded by Greek statuary and Japanese gardens, and Carla would stroll through it all like a Class A *ramera*, a Class A whore.

"Your business finished?" she said, stopping beside the bed. "Your business that's so important no one should hear it?"

"Right now," he said, "you are my business." He reached for her and his hand began a slow descent down the length of her back. Ramón stopped at her hip, then he slid a finger under the leg of her underwear, toward her crotch. Her eyes showed nothing, but her lips parted.

"How long are we going to stay in this dump?" she said, climbing onto him like she was mounting a horse. She held herself up a little so he could continue what he was doing.

"Two days, maybe three," he said.

"And you still won't tell me what it is."

"It's not necessary for you to know."

She closed her eyes and reached behind her back. Her bra fell across his stomach. Then she leaned down toward him until her nipples grazed his chest. She began to move back and forth, back and forth.

"You'll have everything you want. Everything you deserve," he said.

She dragged her nipples across his stomach, his chest, his chin, his mouth. She teased one toward his lips, then the other. Finally Ramón grabbed one tit with his teeth and she went still. He began licking, sucking, took the other tit in his hand, kneading it, keeping the kneading and the licking and the sucking in time with the motion of his finger in her pussy.

"Harder, baby," she whispered, "suck me harder."

It was going to be everything he'd waited for. No more kissing the asses of gringos who murmured over Aztec artifacts that had been manufactured a month before in a dirty garage in Tijuana. No more petty trafficking and all the petty hassles that went with it.

The one nipple grew large in his mouth, and he turned to the other. Carla moaned and wiggled out of her panties, bringing her pussy up near his chest in the process, and the sight and smell of her made his mouth water. It was something he had to have.

He caressed her hair while she licked the tip of his penis with a warm tongue, and just at the point when he thought he couldn't hold back any longer, she lowered herself onto him, but just a little at a time. Pushing down, pulling away, pushing down, pulling away. He thrust himself up at her, into her, and with every thrust he was closer. Closer to avenging the past. Closer to that place he deserved to be. Closer to everything he'd always wanted. Closer to *paraíso*. To paradise.

CHAPTER EIGHT

When I come out of the bathroom, the table's cleared and there's the sound of footsteps on the roof.

I go out on the porch, down the steps, shade my eyes against the sun. "What on earth are you doing up there?"

Gary grins down at me. "Ripping out this vine before it lifts every shingle off the porch." He looks out toward the lake. "Used to be a good view up here, but the trees are getting tall." He looks down at me. "Wanna come up and see?"

I shake my head. "I've been managing to take care of it, you know. The vine. And the roof, too."

"I know," he says. "I just figured since I was here—"

"And the grass," I say to his back as he comes down the ladder. "I was planning to do that today."

He sets both feet on the ground. "I didn't say anything about the grass, did I?"

"No, but you were thinking it."

He looks at me. "No, Mandy. I wasn't." He grabs hold of the ladder, pulls it away from the house, and lowers it onto the ground.

"Yes, you were," I say. "You were always so picky about the grass."

He stands there for a second, and I get ready for things to go the way they always used to. "Yeah," he says. "I guess I was kind of a pain in the ass, huh?" Then he picks up the ladder and carries it toward the corner of the house. Over his shoulder he says, "I'll put this away, and then we can go."

I watch him disappear behind the lilac bush, mad at myself. Because I don't know why I just did that, why I tried to get his goat.

"Wanna be sprayed?" He reappears around the side of the house. He's holding a green-and-white can of bug repellent.

"Yes," I say. "Please." I cover my face with my hands, and smell the false sweet scent of it, feel the cool mist settling on my hair and my ears and the backs of my hands. He gives me the can when he's finished and I do him. It's his shoulders, the way they stretch at the cloth in his shirt, that used to get me feeling all hot and spiky. I keep my eyes on the back of his head. "Well, let's go." I toss the can at the porch and miss.

Ringo rushes over and paws at it, picks it up, and drops it.

For a while, we walk along in silence.

"So how's things, Mandy?"

"Oh, things are okay, things are good." I snatch a leaf off a bush. "How about you?"

"About the same. Busy at the airfield. Not a lot of time for much else."

I fold the leaf around and around itself, try to think

of something to say to keep the silence from coming back. "How's the Harley?"

"Don't have it anymore. I sold it."

I look over at him. "You sold your Harley?"

"Yup." He picks up a stone and wings it at a tree. There's a nice satisfying *whup* when it hits. "It got to the point where I was looking at it a lot more than I was riding it." He shrugs. "So how's work? You still designing jewelry for Mr. Minimind?"

"Minican," I said, "and, yes, I'm still working there." He never liked Mr. Minican, despite the fact that he never met the man. "I'm working on a new line right now. Australian designs. You know—kangaroos, koala bears, aboriginal symbols that are about a zillion years old."

"Really," he says.

"Actually, they were sacred. The symbols. Never supposed to be seen by outsiders, because if they were, then the aborigines believed terrible things would happen to them."

"To the outsiders?"

"To the aborigines." I kick a branch off my side of the path. "Which, I guess, is exactly what did happen."

I catch sight of the lake sparkling through the trees, and something about being out here, surrounded by blue water and tall pines and clear sky, makes me feel a little high, a little reckless. "I change them," I say.

"Change what?"

"The symbols. Very slightly. But enough."

"Why?"

"Because that way, I change them into something that doesn't mean anything to anyone."

I can feel him looking at me. He smiles a little when I glance at him. "You're nuts," he says.

We come to a narrow part of the trail and he goes first.

"Well, how would you like it," I say to his back, "if you had something that meant a lot to you—it meant your mother and your father and your ancestors and your children. It meant how and why you lived your life. Maybe it even meant where you were going when you died." I can't see his face, but by the back of his head, I can tell he's listening.

"Take your Harley. Your ex-Harley. Something you cared about almost more than anything else in the world. And imagine that some day these people come around who've never seen a bike in their lives. They don't know what it's for, or how to use it, or how to take care of it. And they never will. But since they don't have anything like it back home, what they do is take it apart and carry all the pieces off. And before you know it, you've got little kids playing jacks with your fuel injectors. And their mothers are wearing shiny pieces of the engine in their ears and on their belts. And their fathers are using your accelerator cables for tying up the garbage and your chromium handlebars to mix cement. Not to mention their dogs chewing on your three-hundred-dollar leather seat."

He doesn't say anything for a second, then, "You *are* nuts, you know."

We get to the part of the path where it dips down close by the water and stop to look at the lake.

"Remember the time we went sailing at three o'clock in the morning?" he says.

"And the mast broke."

"And the wind was blowing the wrong way."

"And we had to paddle with our hands for three hours to get back to shore."

"It was great," he says.

That's another thing he's always been good at—besides changing the subject when it's not to his liking—seeing things the way he wants them to be instead of the way they really are. Were.

"It was October, Gary. And we were soaked and it was freezing and we ended up having to walk halfway back around the lake in pitch-dark. And three days later I came down with pneumonia."

He frowns. "Oh, yeah, I forgot about that."

I watch a heron flap its way low across the water toward the opposite shore and wonder why my feelings keep hopping out of neutral. Why I can't just focus on the guy who goes to see my mother. The guy who wouldn't start a fight back there. The guy who made me breakfast and washed the dishes and brought me a tissue so I could blow my nose. Focus on all that, and forget coming home early on July 14, four years ago, from a jewelry convention in Reno, Nevada, and finding myself face-to-face with a woman I'd never seen before taking a shower in my bathroom.

Ringo starts making little noises that mean his patience is about worn-out. We start walking side by side again because the path is wider here.

"So what else do you do, Mandy?" he says. "Besides sabotaging your work."

"I don't know." I grab a pine branch and let it run

through my fingers. "The usual. Pay the bills. De-flea Ringo. Go to a movie occasionally."

He stops and looks up, points.

There's a hawk making circles high above us in that wide blue sky. And watching it, I feel some of the tightness inside me give.

"If we could only use currents that way," he says.

Gary has a preoccupation with wind and air and speed. It's why he loves getting up every morning and going to work. Because his work is flying and jumping and hang gliding and teaching other people just as crazy as he is to do all those same things.

The hawk shrieks and goes off in an arc that takes it out of sight.

"Not alone, I hear," he says.

I look at him. "Huh?"

"Go to the movies. I hear you don't go alone."

"Hear from whom?"

"Oh, I don't know. People. No, not people. Me. I saw you once. In the theater lobby. You were with a guy." He nods. "He looked like, uh, like a nice guy. Neat."

"You mean because he wasn't wearing jeans that were all out at the knees and a Grateful Dead T-shirt?"

He laughs, as though it pleases him that someone else remembers that T-shirt, too.

"Real, real neat?" I ask.

He thinks about it for a second. "Yeah. Real real."

"Carter," I say. "Carter was one of my next big mistakes. After you."

"Funny, he didn't look like the kind of guy who'd make one."

"I said *my* mistake, Gary. Carter is just mistak*en*."

The path narrows again, and we go single file for a while, not talking, and then it veers off to the right, away from the water, toward the picnic tables and the campground. The campground is where we used to come when we first started going out. It's where we made love for the first time, inside Gary's brother's brand-new sleeping bag.

The path widens and forks, and Ringo runs down the right fork about ten feet, toward the campground, stops, looks back at us with his tongue hanging out. We take the left fork, down toward the lake, and you can hear him coming from behind. He passes us at a run. He always has to be out ahead.

"So who is this Carter?"

"Carter's a CPA."

"I thought they weren't supposed to be mistaken."

"No," I say. "They're not supposed to make mistakes, but they're as entirely free to be mistaken as anyone else."

He laughs. "Okay," he says. "Then exactly what is he mistaken about?"

"Well, you have to understand that when I first met him, I thought he was exactly what I was looking for. I mean, he was neat. And he was thoughtful. And he was always on time—always. And he sent me flowers after every date."

He stops for a second and kicks a stone into the woods.

"For a while I thought I'd fallen into the best bit of luck I'd had in a long time. And then he asked me to go away with him for a weekend."

"That was bad?"

"No. That was good. The asking was good. It was the weekend that turned out bad."

He looks at me. "Bad how?"

"Not the way you're thinking." He stops, and I walk on ahead of him.

"So now you're going to tell me what I'm thinking again? Why do you do that?"

"Do you want to hear this or not?" I say over my shoulder.

He catches up with me. His hands are in his pockets. "I'm listening."

"So we end up going way out of the city. It must have taken four hours to get there, to this house, where, it turns out, a group of his friends are waiting. And at first it seems like a party, I mean there's food and music, but what they're really all waiting for, it turns out, what Carter's waiting for, what I'm supposed to be waiting for, is the end of the world."

For a few seconds he doesn't say anything, then, "The end of the world? You mean like . . ." He slaps his hands together.

I nod.

He laughs.

"It wasn't all that funny," I say. "I mean, there I am with all these people talking about being raptured—"

"And you went out with this guy?"

"This guy," I say, "had never jumped out of a plane in his life. He'd never crashed a hang glider into the side of a mountain, never driven down I-98 at 135 miles per hour just for the hell of it. And he also never showed up at my place with four broken fingers because he'd punched a hole through his front door."

He looks at his hand, opens and closes his fist. "I always know when it's going to rain now," he says.

We come out of a stand of straggly pines, onto a little beach. The lake spreads out on either side as far as you can see, and we look at it for a while before we start across the sand toward a wooden dock that juts out into the water about twelve feet.

"So, how about you?" I ask. "How did you meet Jennifer?"

He shrugs. "She came into the hangar a few months ago for jumping lessons."

"That's good," I say. "I mean, that she likes to do that stuff. So you can do it together."

"Yeah, well. You don't have to do everything together."

"A couple of things in common helps."

"*We* had things in common," he says.

"The only thing we had in common is that we both looked forward to my business trips."

The words sort of hang there echoing in the air for a while, and I don't know who's more surprised that I said them, me or Gary.

"Listen," I say, "I have no idea why I said that. Because it doesn't matter anymore, Gary. Really."

"Like hell you don't and like hell it doesn't."

His eyes are dark and his jaw is flexed, and I spin around to leave, because I don't want to get into this out here. I don't want to get into this at all.

"Oh no . . ." He grabs my arm. "You're not going to walk off like that, Mandy, not again. Like it's not even worth discussing. Like all you just said to me was, 'Isn't it a nice day.' "

I jerk my arm away. Suddenly I'm shaking. "Well, it's not a nice day! And last night was not a nice night! And that night four years ago was even worse! You and your women!"

"Once!" he yells. "It happened once!"

"How many opportunities did you want? How many times was I supposed to let you rip my heart out?"

"Rip your heart out? Is that what I did? Because, you know, you could have fooled me. The way you didn't say a word. Like you didn't give a damn. Just walked out and never came back. As though that's what you'd been planning to do all along."

"*I* didn't give a damn? *Me?* After what you did? You—"

But words aren't enough. And I'm not expecting to do it, and he's not expecting me to do it, and maybe that's why, when I shove him, he doesn't even try to save himself. He just goes right over the end of the dock into the water.

He hits with a huge noisy splash and disappears for about five seconds. Ringo cocks his head over the end of the dock and whimpers. Then Gary reappears, stands up in water up to his neck, shaking his head, rubbing the water out of his eyes.

Once I know he's all right, I walk over to the other side of the dock and stand there looking across the lake. I don't know how I feel. Everything's a jumble. Part of me can't believe I did it, part of me's glad. Part of me wants to laugh and part of me wants to cry.

I hear him pull himself back onto the dock, hear him sigh. After a while he comes over and stands next to me.

"Did that make you feel better?" he says. He's dripping a dark gray puddle onto the bleached wood.

"I don't know," I say. "Maybe. I guess so."

"Well . . ." He shakes some water out of his hair. "I hope it did." He sneezes.

"You need to get dried off."

"It's warm," he says. "I'll dry."

"We should go back."

He nods. "Yeah."

We head back in total silence.

CHAPTER NINE

After a few minutes I've decided that although Gary deserved to be pushed off the end of a dock four years ago, he didn't deserve it today. I listen to his sneakers squishing along behind me. I stop and turn around. His hair is nearly dry, but his clothes are soaked and dripping.

"That was a rotten thing to do," I say. "And I'm sorry." He doesn't say anything, just his expression changes a little, as though he's waiting for me to continue. But I have no idea what else I can add, so I turn back around and head for the boat dock in front of the cabin because I feel the need for some space around me. And I want to be alone.

But I'm not. As soon as I sit down on the dock, Gary sits down beside me on one side and Ringo on the other.

Ringo licks my ear.

"You know," Gary says, "sometimes I still wake up in the morning and turn over expecting you to be there. But you're not, and then the whole thing goes through my head again from start to finish."

A fish rises to the surface about three feet away and

disappears. It leaves a ring on the top of the water that gives both of us something to watch.

"It was a hell of a bad finish," he says. "But it's not like I didn't care, Mandy. It's more like I didn't think. And I've paid for it just as much as you. More, maybe. You had it done to you, but I *did* it. I'm the one who's responsible for the whole damn thing. And if I could take it back, I would. But I can't. So all I can say is it was stupid, I was stupid, the whole thing was stupid. And I'm sorry. Not like I haven't said it already."

If I shift myself just a little bit toward Ringo, I'm covering exactly three of the dock's boards with my butt. Somehow, it feels important to be sitting perfectly centered on those three boards instead of sitting imperfectly centered on four. Ringo licks my ear again.

"The thing is, Mandy, it happened four years ago. Four years. And when you deep-sixed me back there, it seemed more like four minutes."

I tear a splinter off the board next to my leg and Ringo sniffs at it. "So what are you saying, Gary? That I should be able to handle it better by now? That I should be able to say, 'Hey, Gary, remember the time I walked in on you and whatever-her-name-was and you were both so surprised?' That I should be able to say it the same way I can say, 'Hey, Gary, remember the time we went to Quebec and the car ran out of gas?' Is that what you mean?"

He sighs. "No."

"I thought it was all gone," I say. "I really did. I mean, I haven't been going around thinking about you every day for four years."

Off to our left a flock of crows starts making a racket. They fly off one at a time from the top of one tree to another, then one at a time back again. Making a racket over nothing. Like they usually do.

I toss the splinter into the water and it bobs along the surface. Ringo goes to the edge of the dock and watches it, stretches his nose toward it, and looks like he's considering whether it might or might not be a good idea to jump in and bring it back where it belongs.

"Did your mother have a pressure cooker?"

He looks at me. "A what?"

"A pressure cooker. You know, one of those heavy steel pots, with a lid that sets on tight and a little round pressure gauge that rocks on top of the lid?"

"Yeah," he says, "I guess she did. Why?"

I turn toward him. I find that looking at him isn't hard any more. In a way, it's almost like seeing him with new eyes. Eyes that don't see what he used to be, or what I've made him out to be, but eyes that see what he is. I notice the etched airplanes on the metal buttons of the shirt he's wearing, and the way his hair still hangs down over his collar because he hates going to the barber. And that his nose is peeling the same way it always used to all summer and fall, and that his eyes are greener than I remember and that they have laugh lines at the corners now even when he's not laughing.

"They cook the heck out of food, you know," I say. "I mean, the first time I had a crunchy piece of broccoli, I didn't even know what it was."

"Really," he says.

"But the thing is, that's what I felt like."

"A piece of broccoli?"

"A pressure cooker, Gary. The steam's supposed to come out of it in little bursts the whole time it's cooking. And then there's this one last sigh when you open the lid. But if the steam stays inside, and then you open the lid and let it all out at once, then what you have is an explosion. It hits the ceiling. Boom. And I think that's what happened back there." I pick up a pebble and toss it in the water. "Anyway, I think the lid's off now."

"Good," he says. "That's good."

We sit there for half an hour, talking about things that don't matter—that I'm thinking about buying a new car, that the Italian restaurant we used to go to has changed hands and the sauce just isn't the same anymore, that Ringo could probably use more exercise than he gets.

"You could come over and take him out, you know," I say. "He's cooped up in that backyard most of the day. If you drive by and want to take him for a walk, it's perfectly fine with me."

"Or if you want to go away," he says, "you know, for a weekend or a week, whatever, I could take him. No reason to have to pay for a kennel." He leans sideways and reaches into his back pocket for his wallet. He takes out a wet card and hands it to me. NEW JEFFERSON AIRPORT, it says. SMALL AIRCRAFT, GLIDERS, PARACHUTE JUMPING, HOT AIR BALLOONS. GARY BASCH, OWNER. "That's my home address down in the left-hand corner, and my number."

"Wilson Circle?" I say. "Isn't that Gus's place?"

Gus was best man at our wedding. He was born and raised in Lone Oak, Texas, and he's the one whose idea it was to have everyone show up for a chivaree at the motel on our wedding night. Except by then, they were all so drunk they ended up at the wrong motel and spent the rest of the night in jail for being drunk and disorderly and resisting arrest.

"Gus went to Alaska," he says. "He's been hauling fish for two years. I bought his property."

"That place with the purple shutters and all the junk in the front yard? You bought that?"

"I painted the shutters," he says. "Gray. And I got rid of the junk. I moved it all into the backyard."

We smile at each other.

Ringo starts barking and runs toward the road, and then there's the sound of a car coming and a lot of honking.

"Guess Joe got a car," he says.

"Sounds like it."

We walk up to the road together.

"Well," Joe says. "Just like old times, huh?"

Gary goes into the house, and when he comes out, he hands me the spare key that was above the door. "You better do something else with this," he says, "or there's no telling who you'll find in there someday."

I take the key.

" 'Bye, Mandy," he says.

We stand there, both of us awkward for a second, and then he leans forward and kisses me on the tip of my nose. I'd forgotten that, and it makes me giggle the way it always used to.

He drops down on one knee and scratches Ringo behind the ears. "Be good," he says.

I stand there watching the car until it disappears.

The drive home Sunday night is long and quiet, and I'm happy going fifty-five, with Ringo snoring beside me on the passenger seat and my cheeks hot with the sunburn I got floating on my back too long. But it's okay. It was worth it. The whole weekend was worth it.

When I stop the car in the driveway, Ringo lifts his head off his paws, yawns, sits up, and looks around.

"We're home, Ring."

I lift my bag off the backseat and head up the path, keys in hand, when I hear a car door slam. There are other houses on the street, cars come and go, even if it is midnight on a Sunday night. Then I hear footsteps coming up the driveway, and Ringo lowers his head and growls. I try to get the key into the lock, but first it's upside down and then it jams. I half turn toward the driveway to see who it is, but I'm standing under the front door light and I can't see a thing in the darkness beyond it. It hits me, though, that whoever's coming up the driveway can see me just fine.

"Amanda Basch?"

My stomach does a flip. Out of the darkness steps one man, then another. Ringo growls, but it's not even close to the way he sounded when he had Jennifer pinned. I grab his collar.

"He's dangerous," I manage to say. "Watch out."

But as soon as I've said it, I know it's not going to do any good, because even with my heart pounding in my ears and my throat going tight and dry, I can see that neither of these guys is even one little bit impressed.

CHAPTER TEN

"Bastard," the voice screamed. "How am I supposed to come up with that kind of money?"

Ramón moved the phone away from his ear, then switched it from one ear to the other. The pig, the *puerco*, was spitting and squealing. But the pig was also *muy hambriento*, very hungry, and there was only one source of food. "C'mon, Manny," he said. "Don't do this. Don't make your problem my problem."

"What I'd like to do," Manny hissed, "is fix it so you'd never have a problem again."

"Primo, c'mon. Lighten up." He picked up a pencil and drew a picture of a pig on the back of the motel receipt. He was getting goddamn sick of these motels. He wanted this thing done. "Think of it as an *obligación de familia*, Manny. A six-year-old debt you're finally paying off. Think how righteous you'll feel. How noble. And think of this, too—make me mad with a bad attitude, and I just might start wanting more."

He could hear Manny breathing into the phone.

"Didn't I set you up when you came home?" Manny said. "The store, the cash, the car. I remembered that, didn't I? That you always lusted for the Maserati?"

Ramón was drawing whiskers on either side of the pig's snout, and the pencil point snapped. "Chicken-shit," he said.

"I was going to cut you in on this," Manny said, ignoring him, "but after it was done. Only after. I wanted you away from the trouble. There can still be trouble, you know. Can you blame me for that? After what happened in Guatemala?"

Ramón sat back and closed his eyes. "A *santo* you are, Manuel," he said, "a saint. A fucking saint. And because you are, we'll make the switch tomorrow. In the church, under the warm eyes of your kindred spirit, St. Teresa of the Roses. Three o'clock sharp."

There was a familiar slam on the other end of the phone, Manny bringing his ham of a fist down onto his two-thousand-dollar walnut desk. "Can't you hear what I'm saying?" he yelled. "Half a million dollars you will not get in twenty-four hours!"

Ramón sighed. "Three days, primo. Friday. Three o'clock. Don't be late." He hung up.

When he opened the door to the bedroom, a magazine came flying through the air and hit him hard in the side of the head. "I can't fucking stand this anymore!" Three others came at him, one right after the other, and he ducked two, took the last one off his shoulder. "Are we fucking doing this for the rest of our lives?" Carla picked up a soda can beside her on the table, but in two long strides he got to her, his hand around her wrist before she had a chance to fling it. "You sonofabitch, let me go!" She brought her other hand up, and he grabbed that one, too. "You're hurting me! Let me go! I'll scream!"

"No, you won't," he said. He covered her mouth with his and forced her down onto the couch. She fought very hard for a few seconds, then not so hard.

"Asshole," she said.

"Cunt," he said.

They both started to laugh.

"I have something for you to do," he said. "Something you'll like."

"I'm tired of that, too," she said. "You're like a fucking lion. Seventeen times a day." She pouted.

"Something else," he said. "I want you to go to the airport and buy two tickets for Friday night. Anytime after eight. I don't care where. You decide."

The pout disappeared. She looked up at him. Then her eyes narrowed. "What do you mean, I decide? Since when do you let me decide anything?"

"Since now."

"San Diego?" she said. "Miami?"

"Have you no imagination?"

She studied him, then a light came into her amber eyes. "Tahiti? Curaçao?"

He shrugged. "If that's where you want to go."

"Paris? Monte Carlo? Rome?"

He sat up. He shrugged. "Like I said, you decide."

She lay there staring at him. "You're serious."

He nodded.

She sat up. "I don't have any clothes."

"We'll buy you clothes," he said. "We'll buy me clothes. We'll buy everything we need. But first, you have to buy the tickets."

She threw her arms around him. "We're rich?"

"We will be by Saturday morning."

She hugged him hard. "Oh baby, baby." Then the tension in her arms disappeared. "Wait a minute," she said. She backed off a little. "How rich?"

He made a tsking sound. "Jaded at such a young age," he said. He took some of her hair between his fingers and fondled it. "Rich enough for now, *querida*."

She jumped up and pulled him with her. She danced him around the room three times, laughing, until she tripped on one of the magazines and they both almost went down on the rug.

"For Christ's sake," he said, but he was feeling it, too, the same giddiness that washed over him as he drove away from the church with Manny's goods, that woke him up all night long in the motel that first night.

"When should I go," she said, trying to catch her breath, ". . . to the airport?"

"Now," he said. "And wear a wig. In fact . . ." He smiled at her. "Go as Mary Margaret."

She shrugged, but she didn't say anything. She didn't like Mary Margaret. And the reason she didn't like her was because he did. "If you want a fucking virgin, why don't you go out and find one," she'd say. But usually she went along, because she liked what ended up happening just as much as he did, even though she wouldn't admit it.

"And when you get back," he said, "I'll have three hours of waiting under my belt."

He grabbed for her, but she sidestepped him.

"What would Mary Margaret say?" She said it in her best schoolgirl voice. She went into the bedroom and closed the door.

He thought about the cotton panties, the bra like armor that suppressed the fullness of her breasts, the white, long-sleeved, silk blouse buttoned right up to her chin. Thinking of all those buttons, he started getting warm. But it would be better to wait. When she came back, when she had the tickets in her hand, she would be too happy to ruin it even a little by complaining.

And in the meantime he would go through the exchange in his head one more time. It was important to visualize, to anticipate, to create what was actually going to happen in the mind first. That, he'd learned in prison, in hours and days and months of thinking, planning, creating. Visualizing so intensely that he could see the bluish bulge of veins in Manny's temples, smell the vinegary odor of his sweat, taste the sweet flavor that would come into his mouth at the moment of Manny's atonement.

He went into the bedroom and sat on the bed. The bathroom door was shut, and he could hear the shower running. He picked up the notebook lying on the bedside table, flipped it open, and pulled the pencil out of the spiral binding. He started making another set of checks next to each item on the list. At eleven o'clock they would leave the motel. He would drop Carla at the airport and be on his way to the meeting by noon. He would allow two hours for the trip, an hour more than necessary, and retrieve Manny's goods from the bus station locker no earlier than two-fifteen. By two-thirty he would be sitting in the park across from the church, watching for Manny's arrival, making sure things smelled right, and then enter the church precisely at three. He would allow three hours to redeem the Maserati, seal the money in the car's headliner, and put it in secure storage for shipment. He would be back at the airport in time for dinner. He smiled.

From under the bed, Ramón pulled out the black overnight bag, worked the combination lock, and unzipped the right side pocket. He lifted out the black sock with the hard rounded form inside and peeled the top of the sock down over the pig's face.

He'd examined the pig countless times over the past five days. It gave him great pleasure that it looked so much like Manny himself. The same black beady eyes, the same jowl line, the same waistless shape.

The bathroom door opened and Carla walked out trailing a towel. "You play with that pig almost as much as you play with yourself," she said.

He let his gaze travel down her body to her thighs. They were the only part of her body she hated.

"Go ahead, look at them," she said, "see if I care." She grabbed some clothes off a chair and headed back for the bathroom.

"You're right," he said. "They *are* fat."

She slammed the door.

He sat back, laughing. Amanda had the legs. Beautiful, incredible legs. Little anglo tits and ass, but great legs. And good lips. Very good lips.

He set the pig on the bed. He would bring it, as a gift for Manny. A pig in a pig in a pig in a pig for a pig. He laughed again. Everything was beginning to feel good. Very light. Very funny. Very easy. And even though it was bad luck to gloat, bad luck to anticipate joy, he wanted to feel the weight of the key to his future in his hand.

"A pig," he said. He separated the two halves to uncover the second pig. "In a pig." He separated that pig to uncover the third. "In a pig." He uncovered the fourth. "In a pig." He uncovered the final pig. He lifted it out and mumbled. "What the hell."

He picked up the shells of the other pigs. He ran his hands across the bedspread, shook the sock, turned it inside out, stuck his hand into the overnight bag. The key, goddammit, where was the fucking key!

"Carla! Dammit, Carla, get out here!"

The bathroom door opened. She was wearing the iron bra and the cotton panties.

"There was a key. Did you take the key?"

"What key?"

"The key! The key that was inside the pigs."

She stared at him. "What in hell are you talking about?"

It hit him that she couldn't have taken the key, because she couldn't open the bag. She didn't know the combination. And he'd never left it open, never left the pigs out, never taken all the pigs apart since he put the goddamn key inside the smallest one back at his apartment.

"Never mind," he said. "Go get dressed."

She gave him a look and went back into the bathroom.

He pushed the pigs around on the bed, pulled everything out of the black bag and felt around inside every pocket. The key had to be there. He ripped the bedspread off, threw the pillows across the room, the sheets. He got down flat on the rug and felt under the bed. Then something uncomfortable went through his mind, and he banged his head once, hard, against the floor.

He remembered the euphoria driving back to his apartment, the goods sitting in the bus locker. Then, the key was in his shirt pocket, against his heart. He'd driven home, carried his and Carla's luggage down to the car, then ran back inside and called her. "Leave now," he'd told her. "I'll pick you up in front of the museum in ten minutes." But while he'd waited for the phone to connect her number, while he'd waited for her to answer, the dolls had caught his eye—the goddamn pigs, the goddamn crocodiles. And the euphoria had made him giddy. There was Manny, the pig, and there was Ramón, the crocodile. At last, Ramón was the crocodile. He remembered taking them apart, the crocodiles, dropping the key inside, putting them back together. But then he remembered something else, having a second thought, that the irony was too good to miss, the irony of the key resting with the pig whose life was about to be made so fucking miserable.

He banged his head against the floor again. He'd done it. He knew he'd done it. He'd taken the pigs apart and transferred the key. He was sure he had. Or had he? Why couldn't he remember?

And then he remembered that the fucking doorbell had rung, and his heart had turned to ice before he could convince himself that ten minutes was way too soon for anyone to know what had happened. That Manny himself still did not know what had happened, and wouldn't until he and Carla were long gone. Then he'd seen out the window that it was a kid in a scout uniform ringing the bell, and he'd laughed at himself, and he'd almost opened the door and bought everything the kid was selling. Because what could go wrong now? What could possibly go wrong now?

He banged his head one more time on the floor. Then he sat up.

Carla walked out of the bathroom behind him. "What the hell's the matter with you?" she said.

She was wearing the white silk shirt, the long slim gray skirt. Her hair was pulled back in a knot at her neck. With glasses, she could pass for a fucking librarian.

He looked up at her. A headache was beginning to form at the base of his skull. "I'm going to need you to do something for me," he said, "so you better sit down. Because first, I have to tell you what this whole fucking thing is about." He closed his eyes for a second, put his hand on the back of his neck. "And Carla?"

"What?"

"Eventually, I'll get to a part where you're going to want to call me a fucking asshole." He stopped.

"Yeah?" she said. "And?"

"And right now, the way I'm feeling, I wouldn't if I were you."

CHAPTER ELEVEN

"This won't take long, Mrs. Basch." He nods at the two men sitting against the wall, and they get up and leave through the door he's just entered.

"*Ms.* Basch," I say.

He looks at me. "Beg your pardon?"

"Ms.," I repeat.

"Ms." He nods. "Ms." He says it again, as though it's a clue to something he needs to figure out.

"Are you the person who can tell me what's going on here? Because the two men who just left didn't seem to know much more than I do about why I'm here."

"First of all," he says, "my name is Clinton. I'm with the U.S. Customs Service. And you're here because you volunteered to come in. You are not under arrest. You are not currently charged with any crime against the Customs Service."

I try to remember volunteering. Actually, I don't remember *not* volunteering, but I do seem to remember having the impression that I didn't have a hell of a lot of choice. And then the words "not *currently* charged" sink in.

He pulls out a chair at the other end of the gray steel

table and sits down. He folds his hands together, glances at his watch. "Mrs. . . . *Ms.* Basch, over the past nine months, you have been involved, unwittingly we believe, in bringing illegal goods across the border from Mexico into the United States."

He gets smaller and smaller, as though we're shooting away from each other across a galaxy or two.

"Would you like a glass of water?" his voice says from some other universe.

I nod. The water appears in front of me, and I take a sip. He begins to float toward me slowly, until he's at the other end of the table again.

"I don't know what you're talking about." My voice sounds like it's coming out of someone else's mouth.

"I believe that," he says. "I did use the word 'unwittingly.' " He clears his throat. "Are you acquainted with a Ramón Rodriguez?"

I nod.

"Did you make several trips to Mexico with him over the past year?"

I nod again.

"Did you carry goods from Mexico back into the United States for him?"

Goods? The word bangs around inside my brain. Goods? Then little explosions start going off behind my eyes. Packages, is that what he means? The packages? And as it all flashes into place, I realize there's nowhere for me to go. Because if I say yes, I incriminate myself, and if I say no . . . We stare at each other. My eyes start to water and he goes bleary.

He clears his throat again. "Then how about if I do the talking for a while," he says.

I try to listen. But I can't seem to piece together all
the words. Words like "ongoing investigation," and
"Mayan artifacts." I hear Clinton describe "a method of
operation that relies on involving people such as yourself."

"Your cooperation will benefit both of us, Ms.
Basch." His emphasis is on "both of us," and I nod to
show him I understand, but I don't really understand
any of this at all.

He looks at his watch again, as though he gets paid
by the hour and needs to remember exactly how much
time he put in, then pushes himself up from the table.
He looks tired, but not nearly as tired as I feel.

"Gonzales will give you the keys to your car and
show you out, and this—" He scribbles something on a
blank white business card. "—is where you can reach
me."

I take the card and drop it into my bag without looking at it.

"If he contacts you, if you hear from him, you will
call me?"

All I can do is nod, because right at this moment,
talking requires way too much effort. He hands me over
to Gonzales and I follow her down the hall to the elevator. She motions for me to go in, and we ride down
in silence. It's when she steps by me after the elevator
doors open, that I notice her earrings. They're Egyptian
ibis earrings that I designed a couple of years ago.
"This way," she says. I follow her down another narrow
hall, and then she opens a metal door and we're outside.
The fresh air seems to fill me, pop me back into three
dimensions. We walk down a short alley, and I realize

that none of this is familiar, but I don't know if it's because she's taking me out a different way, or if I was just too numb and confused to register any of the details on the way in. My car is parked at the end of the alley, and she stops, hands me my keys. "Just go down this street," she says, pointing, "and take a right at the end. The entrance to the expressway's two lights down."

I take the keys. "Thanks." I don't have the energy to even try to make it sound like I mean it.

She looks at her watch. "Two A.M.," she says. "I'm off shift now, so I'm going to tell you something woman-to-woman." She leans toward me a little. "The guy's a shit, honey. Believe me, I know. So if you have the chance, fry him."

I stare at her for a second. It's such a perfectly weird ending to a perfectly weird night.

She turns and walks off in the opposite direction, and I hear her heels on the cement until I get in and close the door. After that, everything I do is automatic—turn the key, put on the headlights, check to see there's no one coming before I pull away from the curb. I stop on red, go on green, use my blinker, drive ten miles below the speed limit. The numbness lasts until I've been on the expressway for ten minutes, and then something comes up into my throat and then out, sob, yell, humiliation, and rage, in equal parts. And by the time I turn into the driveway, all I can think about is that if I could get my hands on him, I'd kill him, really kill him.

I head for the front door, for a hot shower, for a shot of bourbon, for sleep so that I can forget for a few hours that this night ever happened. And then I stumble

over something in the dark at the top of the front steps.
It whimpers.

"Ringo?" I kneel down, and I can just make out the
shape of him against the bricks. The tip of his tail
moves a little.

"Ringo, oh my God, what happened?"

I feel along his body with the tips of my fingers—his
legs, his hips, his belly, afraid to, afraid not to. I move
up to his back, his shoulders, his head, and then I feel
it and smell it at the same time, above his eyes, where
the fur's all matted, sticky and wet. The raw smell of
blood and open flesh makes my stomach turn.

"Oh God—how did this happen?"

He whimpers again, tries to lift his head.

"Shhh." I pat his shoulder. "You just lie there, don't
move, don't move."

I grab the door key out of my pocket and have a hard
time finding the lock in the dark, but when I do, the
lock moves away from the pressure of the key, because
the door's not locked. The door's not even shut.

And that's when it hits me like a punch in the jaw,
that when I left two hours ago, Ringo was inside, and the
door was locked and the outside light was on. And an inside light. I know I left an inside light on, too. But now
the lights are off and the door's open and Ringo ... I
stop breathing.

I slide my hands under him as gently as I can, hoping
I can do this, that I can lift him down without both of
us ending up at the bottom of the steps in a heap. And
then I half drag, half carry him toward the car, keeping
my eyes on the house all the time, thinking that none of
this can really be happening. I manage to get him into

the backseat, hoping I'm not hurting him too much, hoping he's not dying. I don't put on my lights until I'm down the street, heading the hell out of there as fast as I can.

CHAPTER TWELVE

"Hold on, Ringo, hold on. It's gonna be okay."

I take the corner at the end of the street going fast enough so the tires squeal. I know I need to get Ringo to a vet. Except there are no vets at three o'clock in the morning. Which means I need to find a phone and wake one up. I reach for my bag, for my wallet, my change purse, my calling card, and try to remember the name of the last vet, the one he attacked but didn't bite, or even the name of the one he did. Except my bag isn't there, isn't on the passenger seat where I always put it, or on the floor where it falls sometimes, and then, in my mind, I see it sitting where I left it. Back at the fucking house on the fucking steps.

"Shit!" I whack the steering wheel. I try to imagine how I'm going to talk a vet into accepting a collect call from someone whose dog tried to kill him.

Ringo whimpers, sighs. And suddenly I know where I can go. If I can still remember how to get there. The expressway, I remember that part. I get on it and hit ninety before the first exit.

"Just a few minutes, Ringo. Hold on, we're almost there, almost there."

I slow down on the ramp and go through a red light.

"Wilson Circle. Wilson Circle," I mumble. Then I see the street sign too late. I stop as gently as I can, back up, make the turn, and start looking for a familiar house. Halfway down on the right, in a pool of yellow light from a streetlamp, I see a black van in a driveway. A black van with a fluorescent hot air balloon painted on the side.

I pull up onto the sidewalk and knock over a trash can.

A light goes on in the house, but I keep one finger on the doorbell and one foot kicking against the door until Gary opens it.

"What in hell . . . ?" he says. Then he squints at me. "Mandy?"

"Ringo's hurt," I say. "He needs a vet. He's really hurt."

"Where is he?"

I point. "The car."

When he opens the back door and the dome light goes on, I see it, really see it, for the first time.

Gary lets out a breath. "Hey, Ringo, hey, big guy, what happened, huh?" He runs his hands over each leg, feels his hips, his belly.

"It's his head," I say.

"He got hit by a car?"

"I don't know. I came home and he was lying like this on the steps. The front door was open, so he could have been. I have this creepy feeling that there was someone inside, someone in the house."

"Let's bring him in," he says. "If we need to scare up

a vet, it's going to take a while, and he needs to stay warm." He slides his hands under Ringo's body and picks him up, cradling his bloody head against his bare chest. Inside, in the living room, he lays him on the couch. Ringo's tail beats dully against a cushion. "You got banged pretty good, huh?" Gary says, probing around the gash.

I look away, and there's Jennifer standing in the hall pulling on a robe. She looks at me. She looks at Gary and Ringo. "What in hell . . ." she says.

"It's a good three inches long," Gary says, "and deep. It's gonna need stitches."

"Will you please tell me exactly what they're doing here?" Jennifer says.

"We could try a vet, but, shit, they're going to have to put him out to work on him." He bends a little closer and Ringo's tongue gets him on the nose. "Or I suppose we could can the vet and take care of it ourselves." He probes Ringo's head, his ears, his mouth, and then around his back and his stomach and each one of his legs again. "Head seems to be the only place he's hurt. And even though the eye looks bad, I think it's okay. Just swollen shut."

It's why I came. Because before the pilot's license, Gary was almost half a vet.

"I need to talk to you, Gary," Jennifer says. "In the bedroom. Now." She waits about five seconds. "Gary!"

"For Christ's sake, Jen, will you wait? Will you just wait?"

She stands there, her face going from pink to red.

"Look," I say, "it's just that the dog is badly—"

"You sonofabitch," she says, ignoring me, "you lousy sonofabitch." Then she heads back down the hall.

Gary straightens up. "Jen, Jennifer . . ." He starts to follow her, then he stops, turns around. "Did you say there was someone in your house?"

"I don't know. It was a feeling. I mean, everything was wrong. No lights. The door open. Ringo."

He shakes his head as though it's all beyond making any sense. "Okay, let's just take care of the dog." He rubs his forehead. "But first I gotta remember where I put the kit."

It takes a while. The wound needs to be washed and disinfected, shaved and numbed and stitched. I wash and disinfect and numb. Gary shaves and stitches. Ringo watches us with his one good eye the whole time.

Sometime during the disinfecting, Jennifer leaves. She stands there for a second, with a bag of stuff under each arm. "I'll send for the rest of my things," she says.

"I hope you have better luck with that than I did," I say.

"Jennifer, for Christ's sake, will you please wait," Gary says. "Can't you see what's happening here?"

"Oh yeah," she says, "I can see it real good. You and your ex-wife and your ex-dog are all nuts. That's what I see."

"Make sure you get the disinfectant in a good big area all around the wound," he says to me. "But watch the eye."

"You think it's okay?" I ask. "His eye?"

He nods. "It's the swelling. It makes it look a lot worse than it is."

Two seconds later the front door slams hard enough to make one of the windows rattle.

Gary sighs.

"Sorry," I say.

"It doesn't matter."

I watch him thread the needle. "You know, right now, leaving doesn't seem like all that much of a bad idea."

"Trust me," he says, "it gets easier. Besides, you can't leave. You have to hold his head."

For a while neither one of us says anything, except for things like, "Okay, cut," and "Get this part right here," and "Can you put some pressure on that?"

"Nine stitches," Gary says when it's all over. "That's a lot." I cover Ringo with a blanket and adjust the ice bag gently on his head. After we clean up, we stand there watching Ringo for a while, as though, somehow, that's going to help.

"So what the hell happened anyway, Mandy? And what's this about someone in your house?"

I bend over and pick up a gray paper package of cotton balls, roll the paper closed, push it back into the kit. "I don't know what happened. I don't know how it happened. And I'm not sure about the house . . . I mean, it was just a feeling. Maybe I panicked. Maybe it was nothing."

"Panic?" he says. "You?" He shakes his head. "Let's sit down, huh? Let's relax." He already looks relaxed. He's wearing pajama bottoms with no top, and he's barefoot.

I go over to a chair. All of a sudden, sitting down seems like a very good idea. He sits across from me on the floor, with his back against the sofa and one hand resting on the blanket covering Ringo's rump.

"All I know," I say, "is that when I got home, all the lights I left on were off, and the door I left locked was open, and the dog I left inside and perfectly fine . . ." I bite my lip.

He drums his fingers on the rug. "How about if we do this," he says. "You stay here with Ringo, and I'll go check out your house. If it looks like it's been broken into, then I call the police." He starts to get up.

"Gary . . ."

He looks at me.

"There's something else."

He slides back down to the floor.

"I already talked to the police tonight."

"About the house."

I shake my head. "Before any of this happened. That's where I was coming home from when I found Ringo. The police."

"Why did you have to go to the police?"

My finger finds a hole in the fabric of the chair seat. It's the same chair that used to be in our bedroom before we divided everything up. And it's the same hole, only bigger now. I look at a poster of a hot air balloon on his wall. The balloon is like a rainbow. Pink purple blue green. Like the one painted on the van.

"I sort of got arrested when I got home tonight. When I got home from the lake. There were two policemen waiting for me."

His eyes widen. "Arrested?"

"Well, not arrested, exactly. I was asked to come in voluntarily."

"For what, for Christ's sake?"

I take a deep breath. "It was about somebody I was seeing."

He leans toward me a little. "The goddamn CPA?"

"No, not the goddamn CPA." I close my eyes. "His name is Ramón. Ramón Rodriguez."

"Ramón Rodriguez?"

"He's an importer/exporter."

"An importer/exporter?"

I open my eyes. I sit forward. "Will you stop repeating everything I say and just listen?" I clear my throat. "Yes, an importer/exporter. But the customs officer, that's who I went to see tonight, told me that what Ramón imports isn't always . . . legal."

"Drugs?" he says.

"Drugs!" I can't believe he said that. "Exactly what kind of people do you think I go out with?"

He stands up. He starts to walk back and forth. "Oh you know," he says, "people who think the end of the world's coming next Tuesday. People who commit federal crimes. People who get you picked up by the police in the middle of the night. People like that."

My cheeks get hot and I jump up out of the chair. We stand there facing each other across the living room the same way we've done it a thousand times. "Don't you raise your voice, and don't you dare be condescending with me, Gary Basch. You of all people. Do you think it's easy for me to tell you any of this?"

For a while the only sound is Ringo's slow, even breathing. Then Gary clears his throat. "Sorry. I want to hear it, Mandy. I want to know." He waits for me to sit down again, then he goes over to the fireplace and leans against the mantel.

I take a deep breath. "He told me Ramón deals in artifacts. Mainly Central American artifacts. Things like coins and jewelry, carvings, sculptures. Taken—stolen—from ruins and digs. And that he brings them across the border into the U.S. and sells them."

"And where exactly do you come into all this?"

"Well . . ." I look at the balloon poster again, think how I'd give anything to be able to jump into that gondola, float away, and never look back. "It seems that Ramón used me to bring some of those things into the country from Mexico." I wait for him to say something, but he doesn't. He just stands there looking at a spot on the mantel, rubbing his finger back and forth over it. "We used to go to Juarez," I say. "Once or twice a month. We'd go for the weekend, fly down together. But Ramón almost never came back with me. He always had someplace else to go, business to take care of." I shake my head. "I can't believe I was that stupid, that gullible. Anyway, there was always something he needed to have picked up and taken back. He said they were cigars, or Mexican spices, or gifts for his mother."

"And you took stuff back on the plane?"

I nod.

"So now you're in deep shit."

"I don't know. I'm not sure."

"Why? What did this guy say?"

I lay my head back and look up at the ceiling. "That I am not currently under arrest."

"Jesus." He takes a few steps away from the fireplace, walks back again. "Anything else?"

I rub my finger back and forth over the hole in the chair. I know I don't have to tell him this, but maybe it's a good way to punish myself for being such a complete asshole. "It seems I'm not the only one. That it's his, quote, method of operation, unquote. To use women, I mean."

He rubs his eyes, and then he goes over to the couch and puts his hand on Ringo's nose. Ringo opens one eye and the blanket moves up and down very slightly with his tail. "How you doing, Ring?" he says. Ringo sighs. His eye closes. "It's going to hurt for a while, you know."

I'm not sure if he's talking to Ringo or to me.

He bends down and picks a cotton ball off the rug. It disappears inside his fist. "So, did this customs guy say anything else?"

"Only that if I had anything that belonged to Ramón, I should give it to him. And that if I hear from Ramón, I should try to find out where he is and let them know right away."

"Do you have anything?"

I shake my head.

"Do you know where he is?"

I shake my head again.

"Did they have a search warrant, the guys who picked you up? Did they say anything about searching your house?"

"No."

He sits down again on the floor, with his back against the sofa. Somewhere out on the highway a truck shifts gears. It gets very quiet. I look at the clock. It's after four.

"Do you think he has a concussion? Should he have X rays?"

Gary looks over at Ringo. "Probably. But he's got a hard head. And his pupils are even. We just need to watch him."

"For what?"

He shrugs. "Strange behavior. Being unrousable."

Ringo growls, a low strange sort of growl that sounds like it hurts, and Gary gets on his knees beside him. He growls again. "Okay," Gary tells him. "It's okay."

"Maybe we should take him in," I say, "even though he'll hate it."

Ringo growls again, and this time he lifts his head off the sofa, strains a little as though he wants to do something but can't. And then a siren goes off like a banshee right outside the door, and I yell.

"It's okay," Gary says, "it's the van alarm."

"Why is it going off?"

"I don't know. Touch. Motion. Sometimes the wind sets it off." He glances at Ringo. "Keep him here."

I go over to the sofa, and he opens a door in the hallway and takes out a baseball bat, then he goes outside, and I sit there with one hand on Ringo and one hand on my pounding forehead. The alarm is a noise from hell.

The alarm quits, and Gary comes inside, props the bat against the wall. "Nothing," he says. "Wind, I guess."

I listen. I don't hear any wind.

* * *

It's the sound of Ringo lapping water that wakes me. I almost yell at him for drinking out of the toilet, for being too lazy to walk down the hall and into the kitchen to his bowl. But then I start to remember. I glance at the clock. I've been asleep for almost an hour. I push myself out of the position I'm curled up in and try to separate the dreams from what really happened. The trouble is, it turns out it all really happened.

"Is he okay?"

Gary glances over his shoulder at me. "Yeah. I think he's better."

I get up and go over to him. "Hey, Ring." He wags his tail and licks my hand. "He doesn't look any better."

"No. He'll probably look worse for a while, but we won't tell him."

Ringo pulls himself to the edge of the cushion and looks down at the floor.

"I think he has to go out," I say. "Maybe we should help him."

"Let's see how he does on his own."

He inches his way over, touching down front paws first, and when he's standing, he looks up at me as though he can't understand what's wrong, why this had to happen to him. We follow him outside, and he lets it all out on one tree instead of the usual five or six.

"Maybe we should just call the police," I say. "Or the guy who talked to me tonight. He gave me a card with his number. Maybe I should call him. I mean, it's a crazy coincidence."

"They showed you identification, right? Badges, something like that."

"Well, yeah. One of them showed me something. The one who drove with me in my car. I don't know if it was a badge. It was . . . I didn't really look at it, I mean, I didn't really see it."

"And where did you go?"

"Somewhere downtown." I wave my arm in the direction of the highway. "Past here. North. We went a funny way, roundabout. I wasn't familiar with any of the streets."

"Could you find it again?"

I think about it. "I don't think so. Why?"

He shrugs. "I don't know, no reason." I can see his face, but I can't see the expression in his eyes. "Maybe what we should do first," he says, "is go see if there's anything to call about." He looks down at Ringo. "What about you, boy? You up for a ride?"

Ringo's tail wags once.

"I'll go get dressed," he says.

By the time we're near the house, the sky is turning gold and the whole night is beginning to seem like something I made up. It's that funny thing that happens when the sun comes up and all those bad dreams you had during the night start to seem silly.

Explanations suddenly start occurring to me—that it's possible I was so rattled by the police that I didn't really lock the door, that I only half closed it, and that's how Ringo got out. That maybe the electricity went off and that's why there were no lights.

"If everything's all right," I tell him, "which it probably is, I'll just take a quick shower and drop you back at your house on my way to work, if that's okay."

"You don't have to do that," he says. "I can take a bus."

"Of course you're not going to take a bus. After all this, I'm not going to let you take a bus."

"Okay," he says, turning onto my street, "if you want to drive me, you can drive me."

"Fine," I say.

He pulls into my driveway. "But I'd be perfectly happy to take a bus."

We sit there for a second, looking at the house. It looks fine.

"It looks fine," I say.

"The front door's not closed."

"Well at least I wasn't hallucinating."

He gets out. "Why don't you stay here."

The way he says it makes me think of some forties film, with Myrna Loy having to stay in the car, all biting her nails and thankful, while Cary Grant does the dangerous manly stuff.

"I don't think so," I say.

"Then you stay here," Gary says to Ringo.

We go up the walk, up the steps. I pick up my bag, which is still where I left it. We look at the blood all over the bricks.

"Only the top step is bloody," Gary says. "How did he get up here from the street without bleeding anywhere else?" Then he pushes the door open with his foot.

After that, I can't get rid of the feeling that it would have been better to have never looked at all. To have just burned the whole place down and moved a thousand miles away.

"Omigod omigod." I stand there in the living room saying it over and over and over.

"Jesus Christ," Gary says.

CHAPTER THIRTEEN

When Carla got into the car, the first thing she did was turn the rearview mirror so she could look at herself. She should have Ramón take a picture of her this way and send it home, she thought, with a letter saying, I have a great job now, Ma, working in a convent. Then maybe Ma would stop sending the novena cards. Christ, with all the novenas that had been said for her, she was gonna end up in heaven so fast, she'd get a fucking nosebleed. She turned the mirror back where it was supposed to be, fished a stick of gum out of her bag, and rolled the window down just enough to push the foil wrapper out.

She looked at the clock. So okay, she'd get the thing out of Ramón's town house and still go to the airport, even though Ramón didn't want her doing the airport today.

"No, too many things. Get the tickets tomorrow. After we have the key and I can get rid of this pain in my gut."

"I thought you said it was in your head." She'd stopped rubbing the back of his neck.

"It's in my gut and my head—okay?"

She pushed the A.C. onto high and headed toward the road. She ticked off the time everything would take, lifting a pale pink polished fingernail off the steering wheel for every hour . . . two hours to the town house, maybe an hour to get in and out, depending on what was waiting, and then two hours back, another hour to the airport, back to the motel. She looked at how many fingers were up in the air. Seven. Seven hours. Ramón would be ballistic, a maniac by the time she walked back in the door. She smiled. She'd stop to eat. That would make it closer to nine.

He deserved it. Fucking up like that.

She pulled onto the highway and settled in the middle lane, set the cruise control for sixty-eight.

She hadn't said a word the whole time he was telling his story. Mainly because she'd been so surprised. Especially since she would have bet money that the old Ramón, the Ramón before Guatemala—the one who used to come around from time to time and leave a g-note on her bureau—was dead. Oh yeah, there was this person who called himself Ramón and looked like Ramón and talked like Ramón and sucked her tits the way Ramón used to suck her tits, but it was all a kind of dry rattle, like the juice inside him had dripped out a little every day he was in prison.

So it was a surprise to hear he'd done it, had the balls to pull it off. She smiled. Ramón had his balls back. And so what if he needed her to help hold them up for a while. That was okay, too. Soon they were going to be rich. "I'm going to make you a real rich bitch." That's what he'd told her. Like she needed him to do it for her. Like it might never occur to him that he wasn't the only

one leaving her a thousand bucks a night. Like it might
never occur to him that she didn't blow every buck on
nail polish and rubbers. Like it might never occur to
him that she bought the paper every day for something
besides the horoscope. Though she read that, too. But
then what else was new? Since when did any man give
a girl like her credit for anything except a tight, wet
pussy. Credit for a brain? A financial plan? A stock
portfolio? Please.

She turned down the A.C. and pressed Search until a
country station came up. She sang along with Reba for
a while.

It didn't matter, though, that Ramón gave her no
credit. She had plenty of time to teach him. He gave her
other things. And they clicked good, her and Ramón.
They had the same itch inside them. To do better than
the lousy rotten ticket they were handed at birth. She'd
traded hers in a long time ago. And now he was doing
the same, making the break from his past in a big way.

No matter how long it took, Ramón always came
back to her, and she always knew he would. She
woulda bet money on it. Like they both knew they were
gonna end up together right from the first time he
picked her up at the corner of Fifth and Washington, but
like there was no big rush about it.

She rolled down the window, threw her gum out, got
another stick out of her bag, and tossed the wrapper.

She'd have bet her last penny on the fact there was
no such thing as "different" before Ramón pulled over
and rolled down his window that night. It was all the
same. Men, they were all the same. Yeah, different

sizes, different smells, different requirements. But they all wanted the same thing. And they wanted it from her.

But then Ramón showed up. And, fucking surprise, he didn't have any requirements. *He* asked *her.* "*Querida*, how do you like it? Where do you like it? How long do you like it?" Like he was the one who'd gotten picked up, for Christ's sake. Nobody had ever asked before. And she'd never forget that he had.

She slid into the right lane and took the next exit, and while she was waiting for the light at the intersection to turn green, she felt inside her bag for the plastic hypodermic case. She knew it was there, but she just wanted to make sure.

She found a parking space five blocks from the town house, checked her face in the mirror, put on the eyeglasses, locked the car, and started walking west. If it was Chico, there'd be no problem. He was too dumb to zip his own pants. If it was Zeke, it could be easy or hard, depending on whether or not he'd had sex within the last half hour. But even if it was Zeke, and his one-track mind was satisfied for a while, still he wasn't going to be expecting anything. And he sure as hell wasn't going to be expecting her. They were all stupid enough to think Ramón would suddenly appear and go home. Carrying the goods in a little brown paper bag, right? That was how fucking stupid they were.

She went into her act a block up from Ramón's. She took a piece of paper out of her bag and started looking at the numbers on the doors she passed. In between, she checked for heads in the cars lining the sidewalks. She didn't see any until she crossed over onto Ramón's block, then practically right in front of his house, there was a black Caddy. And it was facing her way, so she wouldn't have to walk all the hell around the block and come up the other way. She got a little closer. Zeke. Fuck. But then, it'd be more of a pleasure to stick him, anyway. He'd tried to stick her enough fucking times.

She could feel him watching her, sitting there with his engine running and the A.C. on, and she crossed the street a couple of times to check numbers, a poor lost girl, a poor lost country girl in the big city for the first time. Helpless. Zeke would like that. His dick was probably pumping against his chinos already.

She passed the Caddy without looking at it, keeping her face going from the paper in her hand to the buildings she passed. Worried and scared, that's what she wanted him thinking. A dumb little bird flying back and forth in front of the jaws of the cat.

She went past another five doorways, felt in her bag for the plastic case, clicked it open, took out the hypo. She held it behind the bag and turned around and headed back. He was watching her in his rearview mirror. Okay. She could feel her adrenaline kicking in. Now.

She hesitated just behind him. She moved in close to the car. He had an open box of doughnuts on his lap. She bent down just enough so her chest was level with his eyes. He rolled down the window. "Excuse me," she said, keeping her voice a little high, a little breathless, "but I'm lost, and I hope you'll be able to help me."

"I hope so, too," he said, never taking his eyes off her tits.

"I need to find this address. Do you know where it is?" She handed him the slip of paper.

He held it over the box of doughnuts and looked at it. "What the heck's it say?" He squinted at it. "I can't even read it."

That's when she shoved the needle into his neck.

The first time she'd done it, she'd expected a fight. But now she knew she didn't have to worry. He froze, just like every john who'd decided to give her a problem, and then he shuddered, and when she took the needle out, his head turned toward her like it was being pulled on a string, and he looked at her face instead of her tits, and for a second before his eyes went dead, she thought maybe he knew. She hoped so. She hoped when he woke up with a headache the size of New York, she'd be the first person he thought of.

She dropped the hypo into the box of doughnuts, straightened up, and smoothed the front of her skirt. It paid to have a friend at the city zoo. Especially when, from time to time, you needed to put away a medium-sized gorilla. Up to now, though, it had always felt different. Like it was one thing to stick a john who all of a sudden decided you'd look better without your nose. That was business. But this time, with Zeke, it was more like pleasure.

She walked up the steps to Ramón's apartment, unlocked the door, and went inside. Something was wrong. The place wasn't touched. It was just the way Ramón would have left it the day he walked out. And for a second she stopped breathing, thinking maybe they were smarter than she thought. That Zeke was a decoy and they were just waiting here for anyone stupid enough to walk right in like this.

But then she saw it. The pendulum lying on the floor. She took a few steps into the living room. It was in a wide circle on the rug, like someone had put it there on purpose. Like some kind of ritual killing. Broken glass. Splintered wood. The fractured face with its moons and its ships. The wheels and springs and gears he'd spent hours putting together, and why, she could never figure out. "So it can wake me up every hour," she'd ask him, "every half hour all fucking night long?" It's why she'd never moved in, even after it was clear they were each other's only real lover.

And now it was a pile of wood and glass and metal, and it fucking bothered her. A lot.

She went over to the shelf. She walked through every room, opened every drawer and cupboard. No crocodiles. Then she saw the note on the desk. Who in the hell was Amanda?

She stuffed the note in her bag and looked one more time at what was left of the clock. She bent down and picked up a narrow piece of bent metal, and then standing there holding it, with the temperature inside the apartment a good eighty degrees, she shivered, and couldn't get it out of her head that someone, somewhere, was that very minute standing on her grave.

She ran down the steps in front of the apartment, glanced at Zeke asleep in the car, the engine running, the cold air pumping out the open window near his head.

"Rot in hell," she said to him under her breath. "You and Manny and everyone else."

Then she looked up and down the street, and back at Zeke. Why did she still feel she was being watched?

When she got back to the car, she drove ten blocks to Summit Crossing and parked on level four of the mall garage. She went into Lord & Taylor and bought two dresses. She window-shopped for a few minutes, and then walked into The Steak Loft. Inside the ladies' room, she decided on the black silk, and stuffed the white blouse and gray skirt into the wastebasket. She took a pair of scissors out of her bag, unpinned her hair, and cut a heavy fringe of long bangs across her forehead. Then she left through the restaurant's rear entrance. She took the escalator down to the subway station level and rode three stops to Holland Park. The woman at the rental agency gave her two choices—a blue Mystique or a black Taurus. She took the Taurus. Black had always been her color.

"Where have you been? Where in hell have you been?" Ramón was waiting in the doorway of the motel room. He had his shoes on and they were dusty, which meant he must have been out near the road looking for her, waiting.

"It took a little longer than I thought," she said. "You wanted a good job, right? You didn't want another fuck-up?"

He looked like he might want to kill her, but he didn't say anything.

They went inside, he closed the door. "So where are they?"

"You tell me," she said.

"Carla, this is nothing to fuck around about."

"You think after a nine-hour day I feel like fucking around?"

"They weren't there?" All the blood seemed to drain right out of his face.

"They weren't fucking anywhere."

"Jesus Christ!" He picked up an ashtray and slammed it into the sofa.

"That's gonna help," she said. "That's gonna make the key suddenly appear in front of your face."

He stood perfectly still. "All right. So tell me. Was it Manny?"

She dropped her bag on the floor, slid her shoes off, started to unbutton her dress. "I don't think so." She sat down. "Zeke was out front."

The frown line between his eyes got deeper.

"I handled it," she said. "That's why you sent me, right? Because I could handle it?"

He nodded.

"Now the way I see it, if Manny had the key," she held up one pink fingernail, "one, they would have had to rip the place up looking, and they didn't. Two, Zeke would have been out screwing some fifteen-year-old, not sitting in a fucking car with his hand on his dick. Three, all of them thinking hard together could probably figure you wouldn't take the stuff to your apartment and leave it lying on the couch. And four, why would they take a bunch of wooden crocodiles off a shelf? Because they thought they were pretty?"

She picked her bag up off the floor, reached inside, and took out the note. "From one of your *friends*," she said.

He read it through twice. Then he closed his eyes and

crumpled it into a ball. "She took them," he said. "Jesus Christ, she has the fucking key!"

"May be easier to get it back from her than from Manny, huh?" She stood up, undid the rest of her buttons, stepped out of the black dress, and draped it over her arm. "They left you a present. Manny and his friends."

He looked at her like all of a sudden he was smelling something bad. "What do you mean?"

She took the broken minute hand out of the dress pocket and held it out to him.

He turned it over and over, then he looked at her. "They broke it up? The whole thing?"

She nodded. "Yeah, the whole thing."

He kept staring at the piece of metal like she'd handed him his firstborn on a skewer. She started toward the bedroom, but then she stopped and came back to him. "Like, as a favor to me, Ramón? Do it good to that piece of shit cousin."

He turned toward her and seemed to relax. The corner of his mouth twitched. "He's going to pay for this, *querida*," he whispered. He brought his mouth down hard on hers.

CHAPTER FOURTEEN

Gary pushes a sofa cushion and a bunch of books out of the way with his foot. He flips on the lights over the mantel.

"Jesus Christ," he says again. "Mandy, what in hell ... ?"

I try to answer him. I don't know, I try to say, I don't know what in hell. But nothing comes out. Like my vocal cords have been novocained. I look down at my wedding portrait, which is lying on the floor with its back ripped off, and I want to bend down and pick it up, but I can't do that either.

He picks one of my CDs out of the branches of my ficus tree. He looks at it. "I have this one, too," he says. And somehow it seems like a perfectly reasonable thing to say. He glances around, as though he's looking for a place to put it, and then he gives up and sticks it back in the tree.

He pushes more stuff out of the way, and I take a step after him, step on something hard and round. I look down. It's the poker that used to sit in a wrought-iron stand in front of the fireplace. I step off it, and that's when I see the blood. Lots of blood on my winter white carpet.

It's me gasping that makes Gary turn around and look, too.

"Christ," he says. He bends over and picks up the poker, looks at it, looks at me. "Some fucking sonofabitch did that to him." He drops the poker back on the floor. "Fucking sonofabitch."

Like a robot, I follow him into the kitchen. All the cupboards are open and the drawers pulled out. All my silverware's on the floor. There's broken glass and china on the counters and in the sink. Boxes of cereal have been emptied out. Gary goes over and closes the refrigerator.

"Why?" I say. "Why would anyone do this?"

He just shakes his head.

We walk through the rest of the house, and it's all the same. Drawers and closets ransacked. Everything in every room thrown around like it was hit by a tornado.

By the time we're headed back to the living room, my knees have started working again. My arms are full of things—an empty box of Screaming Yellow Zonkers, one Nike running sneaker, a letter from my friend Pam, who moved to Rio de Janeiro last May, a red pen, half a box of tampons. In the living room I look down at all this stuff with no idea whatsoever why I picked any of it up. I dump it all in a pile on the floor. Is this nightmare, I wonder, never going to end?

Gary pushes the couch back onto its feet, picks up some of the cushions, and puts them back in place. We both sit down.

He points across the room to the desk, which has all its drawers pulled out, all the little cubbies empty of bills and receipts and letters and envelopes and note-paper. "They broke the shade," he says.

I look at the Tiffany lamp that isn't really Tiffany but still cost more than any piece of furniture I've ever bought in my life. It's on its side on the desk, a few jagged pieces of the green and gold glass still holding to the edges of the leaded segments. It was my favorite thing in the whole house.

Gary sneaks his hand across the sofa pillow and pulls mine toward him, so we end up sitting there holding hands the way we used to when we watched "Jeopardy" after dinner or HBO on Friday nights. We sit there like that for a while, and it hits me how hard and smooth the palm of his hand is and how familiar it feels.

I close my eyes. I think about the time he talked me into jumping out of a plane with him. How he actually got me to do it, and the way he had of making it sound like a kind of mystical experience. "It'll touch a part of you that you don't even know you have, Mandy. And once you've done it, you'll know something that hardly anyone else around you knows." And in a way, I guess, he was right. At least about that last part. Because it's been almost seven years now, and that broken ankle still tells me when it's going to rain. And it's never wrong.

"Mandy?"

"What?"

"Remember that weekend we went camping over Fourth of July? Up at Big Thom?"

"I don't know," I say. "We went camping up there a lot." I like sitting here with my eyes closed, my head resting against the back of the sofa, the mess around me invisible. And I like listening to Gary's voice. That's always been one of his strong points, his voice.

"It rained all weekend," he says, "from right after we got there till right after we left."

"Oh yeah," I say, "that weekend."

"And I put a tear in the tent setting it up," he says. "In the roof, and the patch wouldn't hold."

"And we left the Coleman stove and the water on the kitchen table, so all we had was cold food and beer."

"And there was that mudslide the second night."

"And I burned my hand on the kerosene lamp," he says.

"And Ringo met up with his very first skunk." He laughs a little, as though that was one thing he'd forgotten. I go on, "And the thing is, he keeps meeting them. It seems like he gets sprayed at least once a year up at the lake."

"Tomato juice, right?" he says.

"It's the only thing that works."

"We drank it. Jen and I. I'll get you some more." He sighs. "That was a good time."

"Drinking my tomato juice?"

"That weekend on Big Thom."

"Oh, right, especially the mudslide."

"And you were a good sport," he says.

"I guess that's what I used to be," I say. "A good sport."

"But not anymore?"

I shake my head. "Nope. Not anymore. I got over that all of a sudden."

It's not something I meant to say, it just came out. But on purpose or not on purpose, the words hang there between us, heavy, real enough to poke your finger through.

"Yeah," he says, "well . . ." He lets go of my hand.

"Whatever made you think of that, anyway?" I ask. "That weekend."

"I don't know." He shrugs. "I don't know what made me think of it."

I feel him turn on the sofa so he's facing me. He clears his throat. "Mandy, how about if we go over this whole thing."

I open my eyes. This is not something I was expecting, because it's not something either one of us was ever very good at, talking things out rationally, in a quiet tone of voice. Especially Gary. Which is probably why I have this image of us living in bursts of highs and lows, hardly anything in between. And even though it's too late now, maybe what happened between us is worth finally coming to terms with. Maybe that's something I need. Maybe it's something we both need.

I turn and look at him. His face is serious. "Okay," I say. "Let's."

"And I guess," he says, "you might as well start with this Ramón guy."

I stare at him for a second, too surprised to react. Then I feel silly and foolish and thoroughly off base. I sigh. "Maybe we should just call the police."

"And maybe," he says, "we shouldn't."

"Why?"

"Because after what happened to you last night, you just might be one of the people they end up arresting."

"Oh," I say.

He rubs a familiar little circle on his forehead with

his thumb, which means it's getting close to six A.M., close to his first cup of coffee, and his body's trying to remind him.

I almost remind him, too. It's as though part of my brain is still programmed. I almost say, "Better have some coffee before that headache gets bad," but I clamp down on it, because I'll be damned if I'll let him know that I still remember how his body rhythms work.

"Tell me all about it," he says.

And since it seems easier at this point not to resist, I tell him about the Russian dolls, about meeting Ramón.

"And did he tell you exactly what he imported/ exported?"

I shrug. "The things in his shop. Antiques. Collectibles."

"That's what he told you?"

"Well . . . I'm not exactly sure he ever really told me."

"You just assumed?"

"Well, wouldn't you? I mean, if somebody runs an antique shop, and that somebody tells you he's an importer/exporter, wouldn't *you* assume that what he's importing/exporting is what he's selling in his store?"

I turn away from him, look across the room, where the two tiny frames surrounding the shells I brought back from Kauai last year are hanging on the wall at crazy angles to each other. I get up, go over, and straighten them.

"I'm only trying to find out what he actually told you," he says. "How he set you up."

I come back to the sofa.

"Tell me about the trips to Juarez."

Just hearing the name makes me cringe. And I wonder if this is really necessary, if telling all these sorry details is going to do any good. Except there's another thing that I remember about Gary, besides bad communication and caffeine headaches. It's the way his mind works. The way he can figure things out. He'll take plane speed and wind speed and rate of descent and let you know exactly where you and your parachute are going to land practically to within a square foot. Plot the shortest distance up the mountain, and how much water you'll need to carry, and how much daylight you'll have left to make it back down before it gets dark. He actually likes to figure those kinds of things out. It doesn't work for me that way. I'm left-brained, artistic. He's right-brained, practical. Or is it the other way around?

I take a deep breath. I tell him. I tell him that I always went to the same shop to pick up Ramón's packages. That the same old man was always there, a very nice, very well-mannered old man. That he smiled a lot and said hello and good-bye and thank you in English. That the packages were always wrapped like gifts, and that Ramón would come and pick them up when he got back to the States. I even tell him that after a while, when I decided the relationship wasn't going anywhere and I broke it off, there were no hard feelings; actually, no feelings at all. "And now I guess I know why," I say.

"That's it?" Gary asks.

"What else did you expect? Meetings with the Mafia?"

"Just tell me one thing," he says. "Exactly what did this guy have going for him, anyway?"

"Ramón?"

"No," he says, "the old guy in Juarez."

"Look," I say, "you have a choice here. You can either make things easier or you can make them a whole lot harder."

We go quiet. I'm having a hard time keeping my eyes open, and I have to be at work in an hour, and I have to figure out what to do with Ringo and what to do about this house and then do it, and I have to face the fact that I might end up rotting away in some federal prison somewhere for someone who never had one fucking real feeling for me ever. Then the phone rings somewhere under all the mess on the desk, and we both jump.

I start to get up to answer it, but Gary puts his hand on my leg. "Wait," he says.

"Why?"

"Do you have an answering machine?"

I nod.

"Then let the machine get it."

"But what if it's about my mother?" I whisper it, as though whoever's on the phone can hear me.

"If it is, then you can pick it up," he whispers back.

The machine answers the phone in the middle of the fourth ring. "Amahnda, and here I thought I would call early to catch you before you left for work . . ."

"It's him." I hiss *him*. Gary sits forward.

". . . now it seems that I have been very thoughtless in not getting your things to you, and that you have taken matters into your own hands, which I can't blame you for. But, Amahnda, it seems that you have taken something of mine in the process, nothing very important, but something I need very soon. So I will call you at work and arrange to come by and get it. Tonight perhaps?" The answering machine clicks, whirs, clicks again.

"What's he talking about? What things did you pick up?"

"Things I left at his place."

"You left things at his place? Like you were living there?"

"I wasn't living there. It was just a few things."

"What kinds of things?"

"Clothes, shampoo, a tape. My waffle iron."

"The waffle iron I gave you?"

"Oh, for heaven's sake."

He rubs his forehead again. "So when did you get them?"

"Friday," I say. "I went there Friday night after work."

"Before you went to the lake?"

I nod.

"And what did you take of his?"

"Nothing. I didn't take anything of his."

"He thinks you did. Maybe he was the fucker who was in here last night looking for it."

I shake my head. "He wouldn't do this to me. And he wouldn't do that to Ringo. He wouldn't have to. Ringo knew him."

"Ringo knew him. Great." He looks around. "Well, if he thinks you took something, maybe somebody else thinks you took something, too." He looks at me. "Where is it, the stuff you took from his place?"

My mind feels all bogged down in molasses, and for a second I have no idea what I did with it. Then I remember. "It's still in the car. In the trunk. I never took it out."

He puts his hand out. "Keys?" I take them out of my pocket. "I'll be right back," he says.

"Check on Ringo." I look around the room, think about starting to clean things up. But there are so many things. And I'm exhausted. And anyway, where in hell do you start with a mess like this?

When he comes in, he's carrying everything that was in the trunk, including the boots I always leave there in case I have car trouble and have to hike five miles to a gas station.

"Look who's feeling better," he says.

Ringo stops for just a second at the bloodstain, then he walks over and puts his head on my lap.

"Poor baby," I say, rubbing the tip of his ear between my fingers. He eyes the couch, and then very gingerly, very slowly, he slips up onto it. Usually, he's not allowed. But he seems to sense that anything he does right now is fine with everybody.

Gary sits down and puts my stuff on the floor in front of us.

"All of it's mine," I say. "None of it's his. I told you."

"Okay," he says, "but what if something of his is inside something of yours without you knowing it." He holds up my knotted purple tights, all lumpy with the things I dropped down the legs. "Like this," he says.

"Oh gee," I say, "is there really something inside those?" I take the tights and stick my hand down one leg. "Shampoo!" I say, taking it out. I reach inside the other leg. "Conditioner!" I hold it up to the light. "Yup.

It's conditioner, all right." Then I reach back in and take out the crocs. "Oh my God, a crocodile!"

"Funny," he says. He picks up the waffle iron, opens it.

"Anything in there?"

He closes the waffle iron. "Look, Mandy, as somebody here just said, you can either make this easier or you can make it harder." He starts to put the waffle iron down.

"The waffle plates snap out," I say. "They're reversible so you can have a waffle iron or a griddle." I show him how to do it. But there's nothing under the plates.

"So much for the waffle iron I gave you for Christmas."

"Birthday," I say. "You gave it to me for my birthday." I pick up Grandma Stuart's quilt and lay it across my knees.

He picks up my boots and shakes them. "I can't believe you left your grandmother's quilt with that scumbag."

"It's a quilt, dammit, Gary. A quilt. It's not like I left my grandmother there."

He pushes stuff around on the floor. "You said there was a tape."

"My Harry Chapin tape."

"Well, maybe that's it. Maybe it's microfilm they're looking for. Or a message." He looks at me as though he's just found the answer to the meaning of life. "I bet that's it. I bet there's something on that tape. But where the hell is it?"

My thoughts pick their way through the molasses. "Forget it," I say. "I played that tape all the way up to the lake and all the way back. There's nothing on it but Harry."

He sits back. "She made that quilt for us, you know."

"She made this quilt for me. You just happened to be in the bed."

"Like Ramón?"

I stand up, holding the quilt in front of me like a shield. "What about that woman you were sleeping with while I was in Reno? Wasn't Gram's quilt right there on my bed then?"

He leans back against the sofa, puts the heels of his hands against his temples.

It must be a real good caffeine headache by now. A real mother of a caffeine headache.

"I thought it was out of your system." He says it as though his teeth are clenched. Then he stands up and walks over to the desk, kicks a box of Kleenex out of his way. "I thought you cleared it all out when you shoved me off the end of the dock. I thought all the fucking steam was released."

We stand there and glare at each other. But it takes energy to glare, energy to stay that mad. And you just can't do it for more than a few seconds on no sleep.

I yawn. He blows out a long breath.

"I'm going to call the airport and tell them I'm not coming in," he says. "I think you should call work and do the same." He rubs his head, grimaces. "Do you have any coffee?"

"No," I lie. "I only drink tea. Chamomile tea." He hates chamomile tea.

He comes over to me. His eyes are red. "I'm going

to make that call, and then I'm going to make myself a cup of coffee. Do you want some?"

I start folding the quilt. I shrug. "I guess so."

I toss the quilt on the couch and go down the hall to the bathroom. I look at myself in the mirror. My mother's circles are under my eyes, and I look like one of those refugees you see every night on the news. Vacant and staring and pathetic. I wash my face, brush my teeth, comb my hair. While I'm changing my clothes, the smell of coffee and toasting bread comes floating into the bedroom, and all of a sudden, I've never been so hungry in my life.

When I walk into the kitchen, stuff that was on the floor is stacked along the edges, most of the cereal and broken glass is in a pile by the back door, and Gary's sitting at the table with two cups of coffee and a plate holding a tower of buttered cinnamon toast.

"Your turn to make your call," he says.

I grab a piece of toast on my way to the phone.

Lauren answers. "Ooooh," she says, "are you sick?"

"I seem to be coming down with something," I say.

"Feverish?" she asks.

"Maybe."

"Achy? Sore throat? Queasy stomach?"

"A little. No. And no."

"Well, you remember how sick I was last month?" she asks. "Why, I thought I was gonna just lie there in that bed and die, and it all started just like that. Sort of achy, sort of just not right, you know?" She starts to take me through her illness, one day at a time. I'm standing behind Gary. He takes a sip of his coffee, a big bite of toast, wipes his fingers on his pants. The crocs are sitting next to his plate, and he picks them up, turns them around, then he seems to notice the seam in the middle for the first time. He pulls it apart, Papa Croc, and sets the pieces in front of him on the table. He takes another sip of coffee, another bite of toast.

"And don't even *ask* what my head felt like," Lauren's saying. "I mean, my eyes were swollen out to here."

He takes apart the next croc, Mama, and sets the two halves next to her husband. He holds the first little croc in one hand while he drinks more coffee, then he puts his cup down and pulls it apart. Little Croc Two is my favorite, all in pink, with a sweet little girl look on her little reptile face.

"The doctor said he'd never seen anything like it before."

"Really?" I say to Lauren.

He pulls Little Croc Two apart, and there's Little Croc Three, painted in old-fashioned britches and a sailor cap.

"Can you imagine what that felt like? Amanda? Hello?"

"Oh. No, Lauren, no, I just can't imagine."

It's Baby Croc that makes you realize just how much artistry goes into these things. Tiny and perfect and painted with the finest, lightest brush strokes you can imagine. Gary finishes his coffee, gets up, and pours himself another mug. He eats another half piece of toast, takes a short sip of the hot coffee, and then pulls Little Croc Three apart. Inside, there is no Baby Croc. There's only a key, which falls out onto his toast when he turns the halves of Little Croc Three upside down.

He picks it up and looks at it, turns it over, looks at it again. Then he turns in his chair and holds it up to me.

" 'Bye Lauren," I say, and hang up in the middle of her swollen liver.

Our eyes move from the key to each other, then back to the key.

"Is it yours?" he asks.

I shake my head. I sit down at the table. He props the key up against the plate of toast, and we just stare at it.

CHAPTER FIFTEEN

"There's a number on it."

"Yeah, ninety-three," Gary says. It's his turn to pick it up and stare at it.

"The not-very-important thing Ramón was talking about in his message," I say.

"The hardly-matters-if-I-ever-get-it-back thing."

"The throw-it-away-if-you-want-to-cuz-it's-of-no-value-to-anybody thing."

We look at each other and giggle. We're just on the edge of giddy. But then the smile fades from his face.

"Maybe the thing Ringo got his head bashed in over."

"You think that's what they were looking for?"

"They were goddamn looking for something."

"Do you think that's what the customs officials are after?"

He shakes his head. "I don't know. There's something funny about that. Something that bothers me about the Customs thing."

He leans back and pushes the front legs of his chair off the ground, rocks back and forth on the back legs.

I used to hate it when he did that. "It ruins the legs," I used to say, but I don't say anything now.

"First of all," Gary continues, "why were they waiting for you at midnight? Why the middle of the night? They didn't arrest you. They didn't charge you. They told you, in fact, that they thought you'd been duped. And you had nothing to tell them, but they didn't seem to expect that you would. So why couldn't the whole thing have waited until the next day? You could have been questioned at home or at your office. And why does your house get broken into while you're with them? Coincidence?" He drums his fingers on the table. "I can't remember, did you say they showed you identification?"

I nod.

"Do you remember what it said? What it looked like? And what about this place they took you to? Was there a name on the building? Did it say U.S. Customs?"

I think about it. "I don't know. I can't remember." I put my head down on the table. "I can't think about this anymore, Gary. I'm exhausted."

His chair scrapes back, his hands are on my shoulders. "Okay," he says. "Go to bed."

"What about you, what are you going to do?"

"Hit the sofa," he says. He steers me across the kitchen and down the hall. "The guy gave you a card, right? A card with a name and a phone number on it?"

"It's in my bag." I yawn. "The one that was on the steps."

He follows me down the hall; we put the box spring and the mattress back on the frame.

I remember lying down. I remember how good it feels to close my eyes and keep them closed. I remember feeling a blanket settle under my chin. It's the last thing I remember.

When I open my eyes, the sun is angling in my window the way it does on Saturday mornings, when I sleep till noon. I hear the sound of my vacuum down the hall, and for a second I can't figure anything out—why I'm in bed with my clothes on at noon, why my vacuum's running, why I feel like I've been dipped in lead. I close my eyes and groan. That's when Ringo licks me on the chin.

"Ringo." I look at his sad, bloodshot eye, his swollen head. "Are you feeling better?" He wags his tail.

The bed's all warm where he's been sleeping next to me. He's not allowed to lie on the bed, any more than he's allowed to lie on the couch. And now I'll probably never be able to keep him on the floor again.

"Poor baby." I scratch his neck. He closes his eyes and sighs. I close my eyes and sigh, too. The sound of the vacuum gets louder and louder until it sounds like it's sitting right on my pillow.

It shuts off. I squint my eyes open.

"Hey." Gary sits down on the bed. "I guess you two could use more sleep, huh?"

"How about a couple of days?"

"I figured he'd be happier in here with you. That maybe he deserves a little extra TLC."

"Does he seem okay?"

"Yeah." He pats Ringo's side. "It'd take more than a rap with a fire poker to put him out."

I push myself up on my elbows. "What about you? Is vacuuming the way you get your rest nowadays?"

"I got a little sleep. Anyway, I've been thinking about this thing, and we've got to make some decisions."

"About?"

"Take a shower," he says. "I did, and I feel a lot better. Then we'll talk." He bends over and kisses me on the forehead. Then he sits back, and from the look on his face, it's hard to tell who's more surprised by it.

I stay in the shower a long time, till the hot water's all used up and I'm almost feeling human again. Back in the bedroom, everything that was on the floor is picked up. The drawers are back in the bureau and the nightstand. The blankets are gone, so they must be back in the chest at the foot of the bed. Things are in little piles all around the room.

"Do you want mustard or ketchup on your egg sandwich?" Gary yells down the hall.

"Mustard, please."

That's something we invented when McDonald's still didn't have a thing on their minds besides burgers and fries.

It looks like he's hung the blouses and dresses that were on the floor back in the closet, and I try to remember if there was ever one single time when he picked anything up off the floor the whole entire time we were married. "In your dreams," I say to myself in the mirror. I stand to the right of the big crack that runs down the middle of the glass now. Then I move to the left.

Then I stand with the crack going straight through the middle of me. My right side is a little dropped down from my left—my right eye, the right side of my nose and mouth, my right breast. And looking down, that's when I notice what's sitting on the bureau. It's a frame with a bunch of pictures we took in the photo booth at Muscle Beach on our honeymoon. I pick it up and look at it. I smile. We were so crazy that day. There's one of us pretending to choke each other. One with both of us crossing our eyes, another with the backs of our heads facing the camera, one with my chin resting on the top of Gary's head, and then one vice versa. One of us kissing. It was in a box on the top shelf in the closet. It's been there for four years. And it makes me wonder if Gary put it here as a joke, or because that's where he really thinks I keep it, or if he put it here because that's where he thinks it belongs.

"Hey," he yells down the hall, "come and get it."

He probably put it there as a joke. And just to keep the joke going, I leave it right where it is.

I throw on clean clothes, comb my wet hair, steel myself for the mess that's out there waiting for me. But compared to what it was, the place is almost neat. Books back in the bookcase, drawers back in the desk, even the CD in the ficus tree is gone, and the leaves that were all over the rug have been vacuumed up.

"I hope it doesn't go into shock," I say, walking into the kitchen. Gary's sitting at the table, and he looks up. "My ficus tree. They're very sensitive to disturbance, and they drop leaves like crazy."

My wedding portrait is lying facedown on the

counter next to the sink, with three big books sitting on it.

"I glued the back on," Gary says. He takes a bite of his egg sandwich. Charlene thinks there's something strange about keeping a wedding portrait around after a divorce. But I like that picture. The kitchen smells so good, my stomach starts to ache.

"Thanks for doing all this," I sit down. I push the top of the sandwich down. Mustard and cheese ooze out. I take a big bite. It's scrambled eggs and spicy mustard and mushrooms and raw onion and melted cheese in warm bread, and it's got to be the most delicious thing I've ever eaten. "I had this crazy dream," I say when it's half gone and my stomach doesn't hurt anymore. "There was an animal, a humongous animal, a dinosaur, I think. And it was coming down the street, this street, and guess who was being brave and protective and not scared of it at all?"

"Me," he says.

"Ringo."

Ringo's followed me into the kitchen, and he's lying on the scatter rug in front of the sink now. When he hears his name, his ears go up.

"I always kinda thought he'd make a good dinosaur dog," Gary says.

"And I'm yelling for him to get away from the thing, which he pays no attention to, and the dinosaur is stepping on garages and porches and slicing roofs off with his tail. But then it gets almost all the way past this house without hurting it at all."

"That's good," Gary says.

I take another bite of my sandwich. I shake my head. "No, it's not. Because just when I was thinking everything was going to be okay, it gave its tail one last swipe and the whole house came crashing down all around me." I take a drink of water. "I wonder what it means?"

"That just when you think you're over something, you find out you're not?"

I'm the first one to look away. I take another bite of my sandwich and get a lot of spicy mustard. My eyes water.

He picks up the key he found in Little Croc Three. "It's a locker key," he says. "They have them at the Y, some health clubs have them, train depots, bus depots, airports." He sits back. "You know him, right? Where would he be most likely to stash something?"

"Out of all those places?"

He nods.

"Not the Y. He's definitely not the Y type. And probably not a health club. I guess he'd be apt to take a plane over a train or a bus. Actually, he'd probably never take a bus."

"Okay, we'll head for the airport as soon as we're finished eating."

"We're going to look for a locker?" I put my sandwich down.

"We're going to look inside the locker." He eats the last of his sandwich. There's a little mustard just underneath his bottom lip.

"Why?"

"Aren't you curious?"

"No." I pick up my sandwich again. "I don't know. Maybe." I take another bite and think about it. "No," I say. "I'm not. I think I should call the guy from Customs, give him the key, and tell Ramón to go to hell. Especially after what I know about him now."

"After what they *told* you about him."

"What's that supposed to mean?"

"I called the number on the card."

"And?"

"I got an answering machine. With a very generic type message. You know, 'Please leave your name and your number and someone will get back to you.' Then I called the Customs number in the blue pages."

"And?"

"The name the guy wrote on the card was Clinton." He gives me a funny look. "B. Clinton. Anyway, the operator couldn't find anyone named Clinton on his list of extensions. And after a while, you could tell he thought I was fooling around. I mean, B. Clinton?"

"Well, if he wasn't with Customs, then who was he?"

"Someone to get you out of the house so they could do what they did?"

The thought of it makes my insides crawl. "Maybe we should just call the police, Gary. That's what I think we should do."

He picks up the key, holds it up between us. "I'd kinda like to get a look at what somebody turned this house upside down for, wouldn't you?"

I place the last bite of my sandwich exactly in the middle of my plate. "Gary," I say, "you're the one who jumps out of planes. You're the one who free falls, runs off the sides of mountains wearing a pair of nylon wings, and generally flirts with a violent end. Me, I'm the one who used to sit there biting her fingernails down to her knuckles watching. Remember?"

He hits the floor with both feet. "Solid ground," he says. "And we'll stay on it all the way, I promise. C'mon, Mandy. Let's do it. If it looks like there's going to be a problem, if you get any bad feelings about it, we'll stop. We'll come home, we'll turn the whole thing over to the police or to B. Clinton, or whoever you want."

Part of me wants to just say no. Part of me wants to find the fucker who almost killed my dog. And part of me figures it won't turn out to be anything more than a wild-goose chase anyway.

I wipe at a drop of mustard on my plate and lick it off my finger. "Okay. Deal."

He tosses the key in the air and catches it, puts it in his pocket.

"But only because you still make a killer egg sandwich." I eat the last bite, and then he grins at me and makes me smile with my mouth full.

We put pillows in the backseat for Ringo. We cover him with the blanket. He's beginning to act like he's enjoying it all. Like he deserves it.

Gary drives, and we take the expressway south toward the airport, going only a little above the speed limit, very unusual for him. Very different from what I remember.

"We're international now, you know," I say. "We have jewelry subsidiaries in six other countries."

I wait for some response.

"Huh?" he says. "What'd you say?"

I turn and look out the passenger window, read the side panel of a delivery truck we're passing. "Nothing." Just a feeble attempt to talk about something I'm interested in. It occurs to me that maybe things aren't so different after all.

"Think we'll try an alternate route," he says. "Hold on." Then he hits the gas and cuts across three lanes of traffic like we're the only car on the road.

"Dammitall, Gary, this is my car you're driving. And in case you've forgotten, we have a dog in the backseat with a headache."

He slows down. "Sorry," he says. Then he heads off on the first exit we come to. I see him watching the rearview mirror, and wait for the siren, the flashing blue lights, another ticket to add to his collection, and wonder why I ever agreed to this in the first place.

"You took the wrong exit," I say. "This is going to head us in the wrong direction."

"I know," he says.

"Then why did you take it?"

"I want to find something out."

I look at him. He's staring straight ahead. Then he glances in the rearview mirror again, and I wonder if he's actually gotten crazier in the past four years. "Gary, you know those bad feelings we were talking about—"

"I think we're being followed."

"What!" I start to turn around.

"Don't turn around. The same car's been behind us ever since we left your street."

"Oh, great."

We pull onto a main road and merge into traffic.

"Maybe it's a coincidence. Or maybe it's . . ."

"Paranoia?" Gary says.

"Maybe."

"And maybe your house was just a bad dream, huh? Maybe Ringo banged his head on the edge of the sofa. Maybe that little meeting you had last night was really a Tupperware party."

"Well, you don't have to get nasty."

He pulls into a left-turn-only lane. "Let's just see how paranoid I'm being, okay?" We wait in line for the left-turn signal to change. It goes green, the line moves forward, and when we're the next car to turn, Gary suddenly pulls right, back into the traffic going straight through the light. Cars behind us lay on their horns, tires squeal. I close my eyes and get set to be rear-ended. A guy passing on our right yells silently through his closed window, then he gives us the finger.

Behind us there's the sound of horns, more squealing tires. Gary looks from the rearview mirror to me. "They just did the same thing," he says, "pulled out of the left-turn lane."

A shiver runs across my shoulders. "Then I think we should look for a police station."

He slows for a red light. "I don't think the guys who are following us would hang around long enough for mug shots."

"But that's the whole idea. To get rid of them, to make them disappear."

"Right. So are you the one who's going to go in and tell the cops you're being followed? And why?"

I can't think of anything to say.

"We can ditch these guys, Mand."

"Like you just did back there?"

"I wasn't trying to ditch them back there. I was try-ing to see if they'd follow us."

My right leg begins to ache and I realize I've been holding it hard against the floor, like I'm pressing down on a brake that isn't there.

"Gary, this is beginning to sound like you think we're Starsky and Hutch. But we're not. This is you and me. And I'm getting scared."

He starts edging over to the right.

"Now what are we doing?"

"We're going to get the car washed."

"Funny."

"Serious," he says. He makes a sharp right without even slowing down, and we almost hit the last car wait-ing in the Scrub-A-Dub line.

I turn around. There's no one behind us. Ringo eyes me with his one good eye.

The Scrub-A-Dub attendant comes up to the car, and Gary rolls down his window. "Gary," he says, "hey, how ya doin'?"

"Jacky. Good. Haven't seen you around much lately."

Jacky shrugs. "Jumpin's expensive." He grins. "But I'm workin' on it."

Gary glances in the side mirror.

"You may notice there's no one there," I say.

He gives me a look, but he doesn't say anything.

"You know, Jacky, I could help you out with that. The fees, I mean. You think you could do me a favor?"

When Jacky nods, his glasses bounce down his nose. He reminds me of a big, friendly puppy.

"There's a blue sedan, a Ford with an antenna on the trunk. Two guys inside. Could you see if it's parked anywhere near the car wash exit?"

"Sure thing." Jacky trots off.

"Maybe they gave up," I say. "Or maybe you were wrong."

"You think I hallucinated a blue sedan with an antenna on the trunk and two guys who stayed on our tail for twenty minutes?"

"What I think," I say, "is that this whole thing is getting out of control."

Jacky runs back up to the car.

"Two guys," he says, a little breathless. "Blue car, antenna. Sittin' there watchin' the cars come out."

Gary looks at me, then back at Jacky. "Jacky," he says, "I think I'm going to need another favor."

Jacky rotates his arm like a traffic cop, and we roll into the car wash. We pass through the prerinse and the scrub, through the first rinse and the second, but when we get to the air dry, an attendant walks in front of the car and gives Gary a thumbs-up. Gary doesn't have to tell me to hold on, because I've been holding on all along. He shoves it into reverse, and I close my eyes. We go through the whole car wash again backward. Jacky's holding the rest of the cars back, so we have just enough room to turn around and drive out the way we came in. Gary rolls down his window when we reach his friend.

"Those guys are gonna be pissed, huh?" Jacky says, grinning.

Gary nods. "Plenty pissed." He fakes a punch at Jacky's arm. "This one's worth half a dozen jumps easy. Thanks, buddy."

Jacky grins. "See you next week."

We go out past the Entrance Only sign, get back onto the road heading in the opposite direction.

"Told you we could ditch 'em," Gary says. He looks over at me and grins.

"You're enjoying this, aren't you?"

"Yeah," he says, "I am."

"Well, remember those feelings of mine we talked about . . . ?"

"Mandy," he says, "whoever was in your house last night tried to kill our dog. Don't you find that motivating?"

"Yes, I do. But not motivating enough to give them another chance."

We pass a sign that says the expressway's a mile and a half ahead. "Okay," he says. "We can go either way. We can keep heading south to the airport, or we can head north and go home. You decide."

I'd expected an argument. Attempts at persuasion, maybe. Not this. It's not something I'm used to with Gary.

I keep my eyes on the white lines as they disappear underneath the car, knowing that no matter what we do, I'm never going to be able to unlock my front door without holding my breath. I'll never look at Ringo's poor head without that sinking feeling in the pit of my stomach, never think about Ramón without wanting to give him a kick in the head and myself a kick in the rear. I think about my first date with Gary, the roller coaster at Big Valley. Remember how it took him twenty minutes to talk me into it, and then after we got off, how, in comparison, all the other rides seemed dull.

I flip the visor down because the sun's in my eyes. "Airport," I say.

He doesn't say anything. He just grins.

At the airport, the lockers have all been changed. They don't take keys anymore, they take cards.

"Guess we can forget the airport," Gary says. But instead of leaving, we ride up the escalator and take a walk through the terminal, because Gary feels about airports the way most people feel about church. We stop at a picture window that looks out over a runway and watch two planes taxi into position for takeoff.

"You know," he says, watching the planes, "I still can't figure out why I did it."

"Did what?"

He looks at me, then back at the planes. "It."

I don't say anything. I don't have to. I know what *it* is.

"I kept thinking how it didn't mean anything," he says. "And there you were at work till nine every night and going off to conferences every other week with your boss."

"I had to go to those conferences," I tell him. "Maybe you've forgotten, but on a Tuesday I was somebody's secretary, and on the very next Wednesday I was suddenly responsible for designing the whole spring line. I had to work late. And what's this about 'going to conferences with your boss.' He's married, Gary. He has grandchildren. He's bald as an egg! And it did mean something, what you did. It meant a whole lot."

We watch the first plane start down the runway until we can't see it anymore.

"Did you ever once turn it all around?" I ask. "Imagine walking in on me like that? How you'd have felt? How you'd have handled it? How easy or hard it would have been to forget it ever happened?"

"No," he says. "I never did."

The second plane has a big red flower painted on its tail, like a carnation, and it starts to roll, slow at first, then faster and faster.

"Okay," he says, like he's just made a decision. "There are two bus terminals and a train station in Greater Metro. I figure we hit those first before we start looking at the others farther out."

"Fine. Let's try the train station. It's closest."

We head back toward the escalators, but one isn't working, and there's a growing crowd waiting at the top of the one that is.

"C'mon," he says, "we'll take the quick way down." We go over to an Authorized Personnel Only elevator, and he hits a combination on the door panel.

"Is this kosher?" I ask as we step inside.

He grins. "I have the combination, don't I?" Then his grin fades. "Jesus," he says, "where the hell's security?"

I get a glimpse of what he's looking at just before the

door closes, a lot of pushing and shoving and yelling in the crowd at the top of the escalator.

"They better damn well get that other one fixed," he says, "before all holy hell breaks loose."

CHAPTER SIXTEEN

Locker 93 at Callahan Station already has a key in it, but we put fifty cents in anyway, just to be sure. The locker's empty.

"Next stop, East Bay Bus Terminal," Gary says.

On the way there, we get stuck in traffic. Right next to us there's a green van with stuff painted on the side, like something left over from Woodstock, and the guy's playing a Grateful Dead tape at full blast.

"Steal your face," Gary says. He has to yell it for me to hear. He jerks a thumb toward the van. "The album, *Steal Your Face*."

I shake my head. *"Europe '72."*

"Steal Your Face," he yells again.

"Hey, who's the Deadhead, anyway? Me or you?"

He looks at me, then he mouths *Steal Your Face* one more time.

The traffic moves forward, and we drift away from the Dead van, but when we come to a stop again, he's right beside us.

I start thinking about what Gary said at the airport, about me working late, about me being gone a lot. And okay, I was pretty high on myself for a while. But who wouldn't be? All of a sudden I had people in white shirts and ties and Chanel suits asking me my opinion on things—"Do you think this design would translate better in pewter or sterling, Amanda? Would you suggest a three-inch drop for this earring? A double or a triple strand twist for this bracelet?"—and over and over I kept surprising myself because I had the answers.

So maybe it's true I was enjoying it all, pumped up and important and not paying a whole lot of attention to other things.

"Part of me wanted to try and work things out," I say.

"What?"

I yell it this time. "I said, part of me wanted to work things out, and part of me wanted to hurt you just as badly as you'd hurt me. But I couldn't hurt you because you didn't care."

"Why do you say that?" he yells back. "Why do you keep saying I didn't care?"

"Because if you cared, the whole thing never would have happened."

The guy in the van looks over at us.

"I cared, goddammit, Mandy. You were the one who walked off like it was just the excuse you were waiting for!"

"You didn't even try and stop me!"

The guy in the van turns the Dead off just as Gary yells, "I didn't think you were going to fucking go through with it!"

The people in the car on Gary's side turn and stare at us. I stare back, and the woman looks away, but the man doesn't. "What did you think I was going to do?" I hiss. "Forget halfway through what you did?"

"I thought it was going to end," he says. "I thought it was going to get to a certain point, and then one of us would say something or do something and things would be okay again."

"Like maybe you'd send flowers or I'd bake your favorite chocolate cake? And one other thing . . . How could you go out with my best friend?"

"Charlene?"

"Charlene."

"To try and see what the hell was going on with you," he says. "Why else would I go out with her?"

The line of traffic the green van is in moves forward. The guy turns his Dead tape up again. "Sugar Magnolia" is playing now, which means I was right. It's *Europe '72*. The line of traffic on our other side moves, too, but the car next to us doesn't until the car behind it honks.

"Well," I say, "I guess neither one of us would win any awards for maturity."

"You know," he says, "that's the first time I've heard you even pose the possibility that maybe the entire thing wasn't my fault."

"I've had four years to think about it," I say. "And they haven't been the best four years of my life."

He pulls ahead about half a foot. "For me either."

The traffic starts to move and keeps moving. There's no terminal parking at East Bay, so we have to park under the highway and walk a couple of blocks.

"This is a lousy part of town," I say, looking at a stripped van across the street.

"It happens to be where I grew up."

"I know it's where you grew up, but it's different now."

"Besides," he says, getting out of the car, "it's two-thirty." He looks back in at me before he closes the door. "What can possibly happen in the middle of the afternoon?"

I leave the window open a crack for Ringo and lock my door. "Will the car be all right here?"

Gary shrugs. "With Ringo guarding it?"

We both look at him lying on his pillows in the back-seat, under his blanket. He looks at us briefly with his good eye, and closes it again. We laugh.

The buildings we pass are mostly boarded up and covered with graffiti. The wind blows grit in our faces and pushes scraps of paper and plastic along the side-walk.

"This is crazy," I say. "He'd never come here."

"We can't just assume that. Anyway, we're two min-utes away from finding out."

Inside the terminal, he checks with the man inside the bulletproof ticket booth, then turns back to me.

"There are lockers downstairs," he tells me. "Why don't you wait here, and I'll check."

"Why? It's three o'clock, Gary. What can possibly happen down there in the middle of the afternoon?"

"How come all of a sudden you're listening to me?" he asks. "You never used to." He grabs my hand. "C'mon." We head down a wide stone corridor with signs on the end wall. Most of them are unreadable. One says REST ROOMS. The other says OCKERS ON LO ER LEV L.

"Fifty years ago," he says, "this was the hub station

for the railroad." His voice echoes. "I used to come here when I was a kid. We came in through the tunnels. The concourse has been all chopped up, but the place is like a cavern down here."

We turn the corner and stop. Three other darkened corridors converge with ours at the top of five sets of steps, and there's something about those gaping black mouths that don't lead anywhere anymore that remind me of a nightmare. The kind you have when you're a kid and everything bad comes at you out of the dark.

"This place gives me the willies," I say.

"You want to go back?"

"I just want to get it over with."

At the bottom of one set of steps, what looks at first like a pile of old clothes heaves, then goes still, and there's a cough and then the sound of snoring.

"Place used to be filled with hobos," Gary says. "We liked to think it added some degree of danger to our tunnel walks."

"Maybe you were right," I say.

We take the steps farthest from the snoring. The stairs are marble and filthy and dimly lit from the corridor behind us, and there's cool air rising against our faces as we go down. At the bottom there's a band of thin yellow lighting illuminating the rest rooms on our right and the lockers on our left. Beyond that the feeling is of a great dark cave.

"Shit."

I look, too. There are only about thirty lockers, and most of them have doors hanging off or no doors at all.

The snoring catches, stops, starts again.

"Let's get outta here," Gary says. But when we turn

around, there's a silhouette at the top of each of the stair sections.

"Whataya doin' here?" one of the silhouettes asks. "Lookin' for a buy?"

"Looking for something else," Gary says. "Not a buy. Not trouble."

Somebody laughs, and with a spasm of muffled coughing the pile of clothes starts dragging itself off along the floor into the dark.

"You sayin' you just wanna leave, man? Come in and then leave, just like that?" The silhouettes begin moving. "No tribute? No tip?"

"That's right," Gary says.

This time the laughter ricochets off the steps and the walls and disappears into the cool air behind and above us. I start to feel weightless, like the laughter, as though if I tried a little, I could float after it and leave this nightmare behind.

"He could leave the girl," one of them says.

They laugh again.

"Oh yeah. He should do that anyways. But maybe he should stay, too."

"Yeah. He should stay, too." Like a chorus.

I can see their faces now. Faces of boys I've never seen, never known, never talked to. All with blank smiles.

A sound comes out of me, and Gary pulls me tight against him. He says something, but the words don't mean anything to me. He pulls me backward as they approach.

"Listen guys . . ." he says, and then there's a pop like the sound of a cork coming out of a bottle, and the guy with the biggest smile suddenly looks like he doesn't understand what's happening. He pitches forward onto the cement floor, and the sound of his head hitting the concrete echoes in the split second of absolute silence that follows.

"Gun," someone yells, and the silhouettes disappear against the stairs.

"C'mon." Gary pulls me backward out of the light, into the dark, and we run blind for about twenty feet and stop. He puts his arms around me, and it's a good thing, because all of a sudden I need to be held up. "Quiet," he whispers, with his lips pressed against my ear. His breath is warm. "Close your eyes and keep them closed until I tell you to open them."

Behind us there's nothing of what I'm expecting to hear. No yells, no footsteps coming hard after us. All I hear is voices, quiet voices. And for a second I almost wonder if I imagined everything that just happened.

"Okay," he says, his lips still against my ear. "Open them. But don't look toward the light. Look to your left only."

I open my eyes.

"Can you see?"

I shake my head. "No," I breathe.

"Yes, you can. Try."

I stare into the dark air, and he's right. Gradually, shapes emerge. Pillars of gray tile. Gates with unreadable signs. The curves of beds and tracks.

"I can see."

"You're facing twelve o'clock," he whispers. "Tunnel number one is behind you at six. Tunnel two is between seven and eight. They're short, and that's where the light's coming from. We're going out tunnel two."

I hold onto him for five more seconds, because standing silently here in the dark at least has the illusion of safety, especially over where we've been, and probably over where we're going.

"C'mon."

We stumble across tracks, slip through two iron railings, and finally pass under a huge number two barely visible at the top of the tunnel mouth. We stay in the center of the rail bed, on the wooden ties, and twice we stop and listen, not that it does any good, because all I hear is my heart pounding in my ears, and my breath. The farther we go, the lighter the air gets, until we can see enough to run.

A cardboard box along the side of the tracks moves. A man crawls out and stares at us. Farther up the track there are more boxes, mattresses, more eyes staring at us, even, I could swear, the blue glow of a TV. I smell coffee, something cooking. And then the track curves and there's a real brightness up ahead. The sounds of traffic and airplanes invade the silence, and at the end of the tunnel there's blinding daylight and a wash of fresh sun-warmed air. We climb stone steps that take us up a littered embankment, walk through a hole in a fence where one whole section has been rolled away. We end up in the grimy back lot of a used car dealer.

Gary turns and looks back at the tunnel. "Rule number one," he says. "Never go into a place unless you know there's a way out."

I start to shake, and he puts his arm around me. "Maybe we should can this adventure, huh?"

"Yeah." My voice sounds like it's coming through a very narrow tube. "I think that's a good idea."

It takes two Bloody Mary's before my breathing's back to normal. The third one warms me up enough so that I stop shivering.

"I'm not sure what the hell happened back there," Gary says, "but someone shot one of those bastards, and it wasn't either one of us."

"Gangs? Did we walk into the middle of a gang battle?"

He shrugs. "It sure as hell didn't sound like any battle. It sounded . . ."

"Calm," I say.

He drains his beer and holds the empty mug up to the bartender. Then he looks at me. "Yeah," he says. "Businesslike." He looks at my glass. "Want another one?" I nod, and he gets up. When he comes back, he has his beer, my Bloody Mary, and a dish of pretzels. He puts them down in front of me. "It's the closest thing they have to food."

"I'm not hungry."

"I know, but they'll help soak up the booze."

I finish my old drink and take a sip of the new one. "It couldn't have had anything to do with us."

"Someone was following us earlier, Mandy."

"But we left them at the car wash, remember? They're probably still sitting there waiting for us to come out." Someone giggles, and I look at Gary, but it wasn't him. I take another sip and set my glass down directly in the middle of my napkin. I'm starting to feel nicely disconnected from it all, so it isn't hard to talk about it. Isn't even hard to think about. As though it all happened in a dream, or to someone else.

He drinks half his beer. "So it was just a lousy coincidence."

"A most lousy coincidence." I smile at him.

"You still get drunk faster than anyone I know."

"I'm not drunk."

He moves my drink to his side of the table and picks up a pretzel. I open my mouth. "Delicious," I say. He hands me another and disappears. When he comes back, he's carrying a cup of coffee.

"When those guys picked you up Sunday night, they took you in your own car, right?"

I have to think hard to remember. "One of them came with me in my car. We followed the other one."

He sips his beer. "After you finish your coffee," he says, "we have the train station left to try."

I shake my finger at him. "Oh no we don't. We gave it up, remember?"

"True," he says. He looks at his watch. "But by the time we get there, it'll be five o'clock. Smack in the middle of rush hour. There'll be hundreds of people milling around."

"And what could possibly happen with five hundred people milling around?"

He smiles. "After that, if we don't find anything, then we'll give it up. What do you say, Mand?" He leans across and brushes some hair off my face, and when his fingers touch my cheek, the temperature around the table seems to shoot up. I move my head just enough to touch his fingers with my lips.

I miss you, Gary. I miss the way you love me. That's

what I want to say, but the words get stuck in a tangle somewhere between my brain and my mouth.

"I'm going to pay for our drinks," he says. "You stay here and finish your coffee."

When he returns, I can't remember anymore what it was I wanted to tell him.

CHAPTER SEVENTEEN

By the time we've fast-walked twice around the block, my feet are feeling connected to the rest of my body again. I get into the car, and Ringo swipes at my hand with his tongue when I feel his nose. "It's wet," I say. "That's good, right?"

"He's doing fine," Gary says. "No signs of infection. No fever."

"We need to let him get out and walk around."

"I thought that's what we needed to do with you." Gary grins at me. He reaches in back for the thermos and pours some water into Ringo's half-empty bowl.

"You can smirk if you want," I say, "but I seem to have this funny reaction to seeing someone shot right in front of me. For some reason, it makes me lose control." I close my eyes trying to make the memory of it go away.

He puts his hand on top of mine. "You're right, Mandy."

I open my eyes. "Were you scared?"

"Are you kidding? I haven't been that scared since I was eight years old and got chased five blocks by a German shepherd with a spiked collar."

"Did it catch you?"

"Every night in my dreams for a year." He fastens his seat belt, waits for me to do mine.

"You know," I say, "I have this silly idea that we talked about going to another bus station. But that was the vodka, right?" I watch him start the car.

"I think we should do it, Mand. I think we've gone this far and we're in it and we need to find out a few things before we can get out."

"Well, you know what I think? That the whole thing's insane. And if my head didn't feel like a half-baked pumpkin, I'd flag a taxi right now and go home." Then I remember what home looked like. I sigh.

"See what I mean?" he says, as though he can read my mind. "But no matter what we do, first we need to check something on the car. But not here." He pulls out into traffic, and I start to ask him what's wrong with the car, why he needs to check it, but the sudden motion makes me close my eyes and put my head back against the seat instead. I feel every corner, every curve, every bump, and then the car slows and stops.

"What are we doing here?" We're parked beside a 7-Eleven. A UPS truck pulls up next to us, and the driver gets out and goes inside with packages and a clipboard. Gary unsnaps his belt and gets out.

"What are you doing?" He doesn't answer, and I get out, too.

He's running his hands under the driver's side wheel well up front.

"What's wrong with my car?"

"I'm checking for a bug."

"A bug? What bug?"

He gets down on his hands and knees and sticks his head under the front bumper. He says something.

"What? I can't hear you."

He straightens up and moves around to the passenger side. "I said that what happened back there was too weird. It had to be something more than coincidence." He moves to the back wheel well, then crawls along the rear bumper, looking up under the car. He sits back on his heels, then he stands up and scratches his head. "On second thought, maybe it was a coincidence."

"You missed the driver's side rear wheel."

"No, I didn't."

"Yes, you did." I go over and cup my hand along the edge of the fender. I move it along the back of the well, toward the front. "I can't believe I'm actually going along with this," I say. Then the tips of my fingers brush against something hard. I look at Gary and take two steps away from the car.

He squats down and sticks his hand where mine was. "Sonofabitch," he says under his breath. It takes him a while, but when he stands up again, he's holding it in his hand.

I bend over to look at it. "That's a bug? Someone put that under my car so they could follow me around?"

"You don't have to whisper. It doesn't transmit sound. It transmits location." He stands up and walks over to the UPS truck. He sticks it up under a fender, and there's a little click when the magnet catches. "Let them follow that around for a while."

"Who?" I can't make myself stop whispering.

"Ramón? Maybe the customs agents. They're the ones who had your car and plenty of time to plant it."

I lean against the hood. The UPS driver runs back to his truck, gets in, and drives away.

"West Station's the last card we have to play, Mand. And they can't follow us cuz the bug's gone."

"But if they've been following us right along, and they have half a brain, they'll figure out there's only one station we haven't been to."

"The truck will screw them up for a while. And by then we'll be gone."

My head hurts, my stomach hasn't had anything in it except vodka and tomato juice since noon, and somehow this doesn't seem like a very good game anymore.

"If we come up dry, then we'll toss a coin to see who gets the key," I offer.

"You mean like heads it's the good guys, tails it's the bad guys? But who's who?"

"Or maybe," I say, "the thing to do is give the key to the customs office in the blue pages right now. The ones who have never heard of B. Clinton. Let them figure the whole thing out."

"Or," Gary says as he pulls out of the parking lot, "we could chuck the goddamn key in the reservoir and see how big a splash it makes."

It's been a long time, but I know by the tone of his voice what he's up to. That he's waiting for me to come up with something better. Something funny. Something outrageous. If I can. But I was never very good at this game in the first place.

"Or," I say, "we could throw it in a drawer, and after a while we'd forget what it was for, just like all the other keys that are already in there."

"Or we could melt it down into a miniature firecracker and send it to Ramón," he says. "With a suitable message."

We look at each other and laugh. He was always good at this, but he's hardly stopping to think, which makes me wonder if he's had four years of practice, and who with.

"I don't know," I say after a while. "I can't come up with anything. I'm stuck. You win."

"C'mon, Mand." He nudges me with his elbow. "You're not even trying. One more. You have to do one more."

"We could use it to open sardines when the little key that comes with the can's missing." It's the only thing I can come up with.

He taps the top of the steering wheel for about five seconds. "Or we could get good and rich by saying it's the key to your heart and auctioning it off to the highest bidder."

The words hang there, right above us in the front seat, like something I could hit my head on if we go over a bump.

I laugh a little. "I don't think good and rich exactly describes it."

"Yeah," he says, "good and rich describes it just right."

I stare at the dashboard directly in front of me, at the Subaru logo with the seven stars on the glove box. I don't know what any of it means. These advances and retreats. These old feelings, new feelings. These emotions that keep rising to the surface and then sinking out of sight. Or even if any of it means anything at all.

And then we pull into the West Station parking lot,

and it takes the guy in front of us at least two minutes to figure out that the ticket doesn't appear automatically, that you have to press the button to get it; and the guy behind us starts laying on his horn, and keeps laying on it until, little by little, the words and the mood disappear.

We end up driving around the lot twice in complete silence.

"One more time," Gary says, "and if we don't find a spot, we give it up."

About ten yards from giving it up a car backs out of a slot right in front of us. We pull in.

"It took us a long time to get here," I say, "and a long time to find a space."

"Forty minutes," he says. "It should have taken more like fifteen. But they'd have to deal with the same traffic, the same slowdowns."

"And I suppose there's always the chance they don't have half a brain."

"Maybe only a quarter."

"Or an eighth."

We look at each other and smile.

"Do you think we're over the edge?" he says.

"We're here, aren't we?"

We both reach for our door handles at the same time.

He's right, it's crowded, very crowded, and after we weave our way through the commuters toward the lower level of the terminal, there's a last shaft of sunlight slanting down the stairs from the overhead atrium. We follow it, me on one side, Gary on the other, straight as an arrow right to locker 93. Well, maybe it's aimed more at locker 85 or 86, but it's close enough to feeling like an omen.

We stand there for a second, and then he takes the key out of his pocket. "By the way," he says, "you were right about the Dead album. It was *Europe '72*." He inserts the key and turns it. The locker opens. Inside, there's a manila envelope and nothing else. I take it out. I'd swear it feels a little charged, like there's a current running through it.

Gary closes the locker, sticks the key back in his pocket. "We're outta here," he says.

We push our way through the crowd, back up the stairs, back through the main terminal, and every second I feel like we're being watched by a dozen pairs of eyes.

At the front entrance we race down the steps and across the street to the parking lot. From the way he spins rubber backing out of the space, I know Gary's blood is pumping as hard as mine.

"What is this stuff?" Gary asks. "It looks like my old geometry homework—all these grids and figures and symbols." He turns a page. We both stare at the drawing. "It also looks like two dogs fucking."

He's right.

It's dark now, and we're sitting in a McDonald's parking lot, trying to see what we've got, with a flashlight you have to shake every fifteen seconds, because that's how long it stays on before it starts to flicker and go out.

"I've seen these kinds of drawings before." I shake the flashlight.

"You're kidding," he says.

"Not the dogs. The data and the notations."

"Where?"

"In Harris's books."

"Who's Harris?"

"The person we use for consultation. He teaches anthropology, and the company hires him to check our designs for authenticity."

"Is that before or after you change them?"

"I think he knows," I say, "but he's never said anything." I look around the parking lot. "I'm going to call him and see if he'll look at this stuff."

"You know his number?" Gary says.

"Well, sure. We've worked together for six years. Here." I hand him the papers and the flashlight. "I'll be right back."

"I work with a lot of people, too," he says as I'm getting out, "but I don't know all their—"

I slam the door, and then I poke my head back in the open window. "What?"

"Nothing," he says.

I head for the phone. As though my knowing Harris's number means something. Or that it's any of his business.

When I get off the phone, Gary's walking Ringo on the grassy strip behind the parking lot.

"Harris said to drop by," I tell him. Ringo comes over to me at something close to a trot. He puts his head against my leg.

"Okay, good. Here." He hands me a McDonald's bag. "Fries," he says. "Double cheese. Orange juice. Did I get it right?"

"Yes." Suddenly I'm starving.

"There are a couple of tables out here. No people. Lots of bugs." He looks at me. "Oh Jesus, more bugs."

We laugh, sit down, and take turns feeding ourselves and Ringo.

"At least his appetite's coming back," I say. "Mine, too, I guess."

A jet roars low overhead, and we both look up, watching its lights.

"Mand," he says when the jet's a distant rumble, "remember the time we went hiking up Mount Thom? The time it started pouring halfway up the trail?"

I hold a fry out to Ringo. "You mean the time we left the water and the stove sitting on the kitchen table, so all we had to drink and eat was beer and cold soup? And there was a mudslide during the night." I lick salt off my fingers. "Yeah, I remember. Why do you keep mentioning that trip?"

"I don't know." He shrugs. "You were a good sport about it. Like you were today."

"I seem to remember that I got a little drunk then, too."

"Yeah, well . . ." He scoops all the empty wrappers into the bag, crushes it into a ball, and lofts it like a basketball toward the open mesh can.

"It's Michael Jordan!"

He takes a bow, and then the sound of tires screeching into the parking lot freezes both of us solid. The car bottoms out at the entrance, sparks fly, and then it comes straight at us, and for a split second my entire life actually does flash in front of my eyes.

Gary makes a sound, grabs for me, grabs my shoulder bag instead and pulls it right off my arm.

The car seems to slide sideways toward us, makes a U-turn, and then heads back in the other direction. Their faces stay in my mind. A bunch of stupid kids. A bunch of stupid joyriding kids.

Gary stands there holding my bag. "Sonofabitch," he says.

"I don't know if I can take much more of this."

He puts his arm around my shoulder. "You okay?"

I nod. "You?"

"Peachy," he says. "Just peachy."

Harris lives in a house that used to be a Quonset hut. "World War Two," he told me the first time I saw it, "and still kicking." Looking up at that low, rounded ceiling always makes me feel like I'm inside a caterpillar.

"Harris," I say, "this is Gary. Gary, this is Harris."

They shake hands.

"Beer?" Harris says.

"Sure," I say.

But Gary shakes his head. "No thanks."

"So what have you got that you wanted me to see?" Harris sets a glass and a bottle of Bud on the table. I sit down and spread the papers out. He bends closer and looks.

For the next few minutes he studies the papers, setting one down, picking it up again, going on to another. The only sounds are the ticking of his kitchen clock and the rustle of the pages. Finally, he puts them into a neat pile, sits back. "I can tell you what they appear to be," he says.

I lean toward him a little. "What?"

"Provenance," he says. "Very scholarly. Very thorough. Very impressive."

We glance at Gary. He shrugs, thoroughly confused.

"Oh," Harris says, "sorry. It's the origin of an artifact. Documentation of an antiquity that states where, when, and how it was found. If on land, that would include place, depth, type of soil, whether the area was disturbed or not, its relation to other artifacts found at the same site or in the same area. As in this case, a particularly rich find of Mayan artifacts at Mexico City." He glances down at the papers again. "Teotihuacán. That was a very significant excavation. The Temple of Quetzalcoatl." Then something seems to occur to him. "Where did you get this, anyway?"

Gary coughs. "Maybe I'll have that beer after all," he says.

"Sure." Harris gets up and goes to the refrigerator. When he returns, he hands Gary a bottle and sits down with one of his own.

"Well, actually, you see, I have a . . . friend," I begin. "He's in the import/export business, and he's been offered this . . . piece and these . . . papers, for a price, quite a high price. It's a little out of his league. He brought it to me, and then I thought of you. He needs to be sure."

Behind Harris, Gary rolls his eyes.

"I'd tell your friend to be cautious," Harris says. "Years ago, it was finders keepers, so to speak, but then countries began to realize they were losing national treasures, both monetary and historical, and many of them instituted very strict laws governing access to sites and ownership of discoveries. Including Mexico. It can get very complicated. I mean, there are archaeologists and there are treasure hunters. There are collectors who are willing to add to their collections by any means, and there are plenty willing to provide them with goods. And then you have political upheavals, and the fact that some of the most valuable finds are often in very poor countries. Conditions that create a thriving black market." He takes a sip of beer. "Getting back to this, though . . . an artifact, by itself, may have only limited value." He taps the pile of papers. "What lifts the limitation is its provenance."

"Like a purebred dog," Gary says.

"Exactly. The dog may check out in every way, but without papers proving its ancestry, its value is diminished. Sometimes, severely so. It can be the same with an artifact. Without bloodlines, its value is suspect. But with provenance, with the proof of its legitimate discovery . . ." He lifts his eyebrows. "Then, depending on its own intrinsic uniqueness, the sky is the limit."

"Can you tell us anything about this particular piece?" I point to the pile of papers.

He screws up his face like he's thinking. "Mayan," he says. "Pre-Columbian." He smiles. "A unique piece. Which means the sky here could be extremely high." The clock ticks away several very loud seconds. "And very illegal."

"Illegal?" Gary and I both say it at the same time.

"This is not something that the country of discovery would want to see outside of its borders."

"And if it is outside its borders?" Gary asks.

Harris shrugs. "Let's just say that they'd probably be very anxious to get it back."

Gary and I look at each other, and I know what's going through his head. Anxious enough to do what?

That's when Gary points at a model of a glider hanging from the ceiling in the next room. "Isn't that an early Hofsteder?" he asks, and somehow the conversation never gets back to illegal Mayan artifacts.

"So?" I say, as we back out of Harris's driveway. "What now?"

He yawns. "Maybe we should just go home and go to bed. It feels like it's been three weeks since you woke me up last night."

I think about walking back into my house again. About what it's going to feel like to shut off all the lights and lie there in the dark, listening to every creak, every scratch, every sigh of the wind. Wondering if whoever broke in might decide to come back and try again.

"My place," Gary says, reading my mind again. "Not yours."

Ringo pokes his head over the back of my seat. He sniffs my hair.

"There is one thing, though," I say.

Gary glances over at me. "What?"

"I haven't seen my mother since Wednesday, and I really need to make sure she's okay."

"Now? Isn't it a little late to drop in?"

"She doesn't sleep like we do," I say. "She takes little naps all day and all night. Drives her caregivers crazy. She'll be up. And you don't have to come in. You can wait in the car. I won't be long."

He makes an illegal U-turn and heads back in the other direction toward Dayville Manor. "I don't mind coming in," he says. "I guess I can take a little more grief before the day's over."

"Just remember not to take it personally," I tell him when we get there.

"I never did," he says.

I find the right key, knock on the door, open it. "Mama, it's me. It's Amanda."

It's quiet, absolutely quiet, as though there's no one home. I hear a noise from Mama's room, and before I get halfway there, she comes into the living room. She's wearing all blue. Blue socks, blue slippers, blue polyester pants, a blue blouse.

"Hi, Mama. We came for a visit."

She smiles. She opens her arms. She comes toward me, walks right on by, and throws her arms around Gary. He stands there with a funny look on his face, his chin resting on top of her blue hair, and for a second it looks like she might never let him go.

Finally, she steps back. She looks up at him and cocks her head in my direction. "Who's the skinny broad?" she asks.

CHAPTER EIGHTEEN

The three of us settle in the living room. Mama's doing all the talking, playing some tune I had no idea was there.

Everything's, "Gary, would you like some of that nice green tomato relish? I know it was always your favorite." And, "You sit here, Gary, it's more comfortable than that dumpy old chair." And, "You know, it seems to me you've lost some weight. Isn't that daughter of mine feeding you right?"

"I don't have to feed him, Mama," I say. "He's all grown up now and perfectly capable of feeding himself." She gives me a look as though I just admitted to starving her only grandchild. "And, Mama, we're not married anymore, Gary and I, remember?"

She looks at Gary. She jerks a thumb in my direction. "What'd you say her name was?"

"That's Mandy, Mrs. O'Toole. Mandy."

In all her wanderings and forgettings, this is the first time this has happened, and somewhere inside me there's a hole opening up. Because if my own mother doesn't know me, the person who's been there through every breath I've ever taken, then do I really exist at all?

"Now you quit calling me Mrs. O'Toole," she says, patting Gary on the knee. "I'm Sadie or Mama, whichever you like."

I decide I'll never forgive him if he calls her Mama.

"Okay, Sadie," he says.

She starts telling him about the man who lives in the identical cottage next door. How he comes and stares in her bathroom window whenever he hears her bathtub faucet go on.

"All you have to do is tell Rose," I say. "She's the one who helps you take a bath, right?"

"I have a plan," she says, ignoring me. She leans toward Gary. "I'm going to throw a bowling ball through the window next time I know he's there."

His eyebrows go up. "Isn't that a little drastic?"

"She's doesn't even have one," I say under my breath.

"Maybe you should just report it, Sadie. To Rose, like Mandy said."

"You know, she hasn't called in a year. Doesn't even know where I am."

"Who?" he asks.

"That daughter of mine."

"I'm right here, Mama. Right here. I spoke to you on Friday on the phone. I took you shopping on Wednesday. I haven't been more than ten miles away from you my whole life."

"And you can tell her I'm pissed," Mama says.

Gary nods. "I will. I'll tell her."

"You don't need to encourage it," I say through clenched teeth.

"You should get rid of this one," Mama says. "She's got a nasty streak."

"Yeah, well . . ." he says, "she's had a tough day."

Mama sighs. "Oh, don't I know. I can't say I've seen her happy in a long while."

I look at her. She looks back at me. She smiles. "How are you, dear?" she says.

"Fine." I just manage to get it past the lump that comes into my throat.

She pats Gary's arm again. "You take care of him, now. He needs a good meal now and then."

"She's a good cook," Gary says.

"I know," Mama says. "I taught her everything she knows."

Gary stands up. "If you don't mind, Sadie, I need to use your bathroom."

She watches him leave and then turns her suddenly clear eyes to me.

"You hold on to him this time, Amanda, you hear me?"

I'm stunned. It's like my old mother just walked up to me. I can't respond.

"He might not be the one I'd've picked for you, but I'm tired of you moping around like a sick chicken." She gazes off, like something's in the process of breezing through her mind and she's trying to grab hold of it before it's gone. Then she looks back at me. "Uncle Bert always liked to chew on the turkey's tail, you know."

I wait for more. For her to say something that'll tie

Uncle Bert and the turkey's tail into whatever she's trying to tell me. But that's it. She picks up a magazine and starts looking through it.

"Mama?"

She glances up at me and then back at the magazine as though I'm just another person sitting across the aisle from her on the downtown bus.

By the time Gary comes back into the living room, I've stopped trying to talk myself into being okay with it. Because it's never going to be okay. It's never even going to be anything close to okay.

"I guess we're going to leave now, Mama." I stand up and walk around the table, lean down to kiss her. "Let me bring you back to bed."

"Make sure you don't leave the door open," she says. "Goddamn mosquitoes'll eat a person alive. It's the rain, you know. Flushes 'em out of the sewers."

" 'Bye, Mrs. O'Toole. Sadie," Gary says as Mama and I walk down the hall.

She looks back at Gary. "You come back here again, young man, and I'll call the police."

"Now that's more like it," he says, and quietly walks out to the car.

When we pull away from the curb, I look back at the light in her window. Gary puts his hand over mine. "She doesn't know," he says. "She doesn't know, so it's not as hard on her as it is on you."

It isn't as though I haven't thought of that before. It's just not all that much of a comfort.

"Tired?" he asks after a while.

"Tired."

"Yeah, me too."

All of a sudden, I remember something. "Where's the envelope?" I start feeling around on the seat, on the floor.

"It's okay," he says, "I left it in Sadie's bathroom."

"You what?" Ringo sits up and pushes his head into the front seat. I look past him at Gary's profile in the glow from a green light we're passing through. "I can't believe you did that. I can't believe you forgot it."

"I didn't forget it," he says, "I left it there. On purpose." He looks over at me. Ringo's head disappears. "I stuck it under a stack of towels in her linen closet."

"Under her towels?"

"Well, I was gonna stick it under the sheets, but then I remembered how my mother used to yell at us if we took the sheets off the top, how she always wanted us taking them off the bottom, but that it was okay to take the towels off the top."

"What on earth are you talking about? You left something that people turned my house upside down for under my mother's towels? Turn around, Gary. We're getting that stuff out of there."

"Mandy, look. No one's following us now. I'm sure of that, or I never would have done it. And I didn't want to be carrying it around. I wanted it someplace where we didn't have to worry about it. At least until we figure out what we're going to do with it."

"Well, I can think of better places than under Mama's towels."

"Name one."

"How about a bank?"

"Oh right. I did think of that. But then I remembered there wasn't any more room in my safe deposit box."

Ringo pushes his nose into the front seat again. He licks Gary on the chin. I duck away before he can get me.

"We're upsetting the baby," Gary says.

He starts to slow down to make his turn onto Wilson, and all I can think about is curling up under a blanket and closing my eyes.

But then he hits the gas, and Wilson Circle's behind us. He whacks the steering wheel. "Shit."

"What's the matter?"

"There was a car back there sitting behind the Dubinskis' Dumpster." He keeps looking in the rearview mirror.

"Maybe it was the Dubinskis' car."

"There," he says, "there's the headlights."

A chill travels from my ankles to my neck as we head back toward the highway.

"Not fast," I say, "please, not fast."

"We're not going to go fast," he says. "We're going to go fifty-five all the way."

"All the way where?"

"All the way to wherever we decide to go."

I close my eyes. I think white sand beaches and aquamarine water that makes little lapping noises near my feet. I think puffy white clouds and what it would feel like to lie on one and watch the world moving by underneath. But none of it does anything to lift this weight off my chest, and if I let myself, it would be real easy to just break down and cry. "The only way we're going to get away from them is if we fucking fly off over their heads," I say.

He reaches over and finds my hand. He squeezes it.

"Mandy," he says, "did anybody ever tell you you're bloody brilliant?"

I look at him and bite my bottom lip. Hard.

Gary laughs and says, "That's perfect! We're going to fucking fly right over their fucking heads."

After a while the houses thin out, the streetlights disappear. We pass Jenkins's Junque Yard, "Finest Junque Yard in the World," and then the sign for New Jefferson Airfield. When the macadam goes to dirt, Gary floors it until the hangar comes into view. Then he shuts off the headlights. I scream. Ringo starts barking. He hits the brake.

"What's the matter? What's the matter?"

"We're driving blind!"

"Mandy, I spend ten hours a day here. I know where I am." He makes a right turn and puts on the parking lights. "Is that better?"

I can just make out the hangar over on our right and the propellers of a row of parked planes passing by on our left.

"Now," Gary says, "if J.D. did what he was supposed to for a change, we'll be all set."

J.D. began working for Gary when he was a strange little twelve-year-old with nothing on his mind but planes planes planes. The last time I saw him, he was a pimply seventeen with a crush on me that made him go red every time I looked his way.

"J.D. must be all grown up by now."

"Grown up enough to have a J.D. Junior," he says.

"J.D. has a baby?"

"Guess that proves it's not such a hard thing to do, huh?"

Hard enough for some people, I want to say, but I don't.

"Okay, look," he says. "As soon as I stop the car, we're heading over to our left, to the last plane in line. I'll get the key off the strut and hand it to you. You climb in and open my door. I'll throw off the tie-downs."

"What about Ringo?"

"I'll take care of him." He stops the car. "Now," he says.

The almost full moon shimmers along the top of the fuselage and the wings, reflects itself in the pontoons.

"Pontoons?" I say when he hands me the key.

"It's the only one we have that'll land on water."

"Water?"

I climb inside, open the pilot's door. Ringo comes through first in Gary's arms. I help settle him behind the pilot seat, then Gary sits down and pulls the door shut. "Now just pray that J.D. filled this baby up like he was supposed to."

He turns the key. He stares at the gauges. "Fucking A for J.D."

"Water?" I repeat.

"As in that stuff in the lake beside the cabin."

"You're going to land on that lake in the middle of the night?"

"Well, where did you think we were going to go?"

"I don't know. I didn't get that far."

"Don't worry," he says. "I'm very good at this."

He taxis around to the left, and as we come down the

runway, headlights pull up beside the hangar. The light inside the car goes on as both doors open, and two people step out and stand there watching us. Then Gary punches it, and we're leaving them far behind. Leaving everything far behind—Mama and her linen closet, Ramón, my ravaged house, locker 93. It's all falling away through the black air, leaving me lighter and lighter with every foot of altitude we gain.

This is it, I think. This is what real adventure feels like.

Gary lets out a whoop. I let out a whoop. Ringo howls.

As far as I can see, it's like trying to land the plane in a bottle of ink. But somehow he does it.

"Piece of cake," Gary says.

I have one eye open. I didn't even feel it when we touched down, and now the plane's rocking ever so slightly, the moon lighting up the tops of all the waves we're sending across the surface of the lake. "Wow," I say. "You're good."

"Thanks."

He pulls a light off a bracket behind his head and aims it out the window toward shore.

"You just passed our dock."

He backtracks the light. "Here." He hands it to me, and I hold it steady on the dock until we've taxied right up to it.

"We're home, honey," he says.

We tie the plane to the dock, and to two trees just to be on the safe side. Ringo sits and watches.

"Didn't think I was going to be back here so soon," he says. He smiles at me in the moonlight.

Inside the cabin, we pace, high and full of adrenaline, saying things like, "Wouldn't you give anything to have seen the looks on their faces?" and, "We did it, we did it to them good."

He goes over to the refrigerator and opens the door. "It's empty."

"That's because I cleaned it out when I left."

"But I'm starving. I'll never make it through the night." He goes over and throws himself down on the couch.

Ringo walks over and prods him with his nose. "Why did I give half my burger to you?" Then he scratches him on the side of his neck. "Just kidding. If I had another one right now, I'd let you lick the wrapper."

"Soup," I say, taking cans out of the cupboard next to the stove. "Beans, applesauce, spaghetti sauce. Spaghetti!" I wave a box of spaghetti in the air.

Gary sits up. "A feast," he yells. "We'll eat till we can't walk."

"Check the bar. I may have some wine, too."

An hour later we can walk just enough to get out onto the porch. It's suddenly the kind of night that makes you feel things aren't really so bad after all. The moon's outlining the tops of the trees. A hundred million crickets are singing.

"Listen," Gary says. "Did you hear it? Here." He steps behind me and turns me toward the sound.

I listen. There's a loon calling from the other side of the lake. It's the kind of sound you can feel and hear at the same time. It makes me shiver.

He puts his arms around me. "Cold?"

"No." But he doesn't take his arms away.

"We have to figure out what we're going to do," he says. His mouth is right above my ear. "But not to-night," he whispers. "Tomorrow."

He's holding me, and I don't want this moment to end.

But I say, "Look at us, Gary. We're playing games when we don't even know the rules. What about your job? What about Jennifer? We have lives to get back to, Gary, remember?"

He doesn't say anything. I feel his breath on my cheek. His arms fit around me just the way they used to. We breathe in unison.

"As far as my life goes, Mandy, it feels like I'm just beginning to get it back."

I turn around to face him, knowing how dangerous this is, what we're doing, what we're letting ourselves fall into. But it's pulling me in so fast, I can't stop it.

"God, Mandy, I've missed you so much."

And everything about him, everything he does—his lips on my face, his hands on my arms, the way he kisses the corners of my mouth, my eyes, the way he wraps me up, holds me, as though nothing could ever make him let go—is so familiar it's almost like an ache.

"Love me again," he says against my hair. "Love me again, Mandy." It all dissolves into heat and need and urgency. We tear at buttons and zippers right there on the porch, with the moon watching and the loon crying from the other side of the lake, and in the silver light slicing through the trees, I recognize the slope of his shoulders, the line of the muscles in his arms and chest, the way his eyes get hungry and searching and intense. His fingers trace the hollow of my throat, linger on my breasts, float across my hips and thighs. And then he smiles at me. "Is it really you? Tell me it is, Mandy. Tell me I'm not just dreaming."

I kiss his hands and slide them down my body, hungry for that feel again, the way he has of barely touching, barely stroking with those cool, hard fingers. "It's really me," I say. "It's really you." And then there's nothing more to say. Only hungers to be fed and needs to be filled and two people who can't seem to stop rediscovering one another.

CHAPTER NINETEEN

When I wake up, the first thing I think is, Thank God Gary can't see my dreams. But this doesn't fade the way dreams fade, doesn't slip away the more I try to remember it.

I don't want to, but I open my eyes anyway and turn my head slowly toward the other side of the bed. Empty. Then I see the impression in the other pillow, where Gary's head has been resting. I close my eyes and remember.

" 'Morning, Mandy." Gary smiles at me when I come into the kitchen. Ringo walks over and licks my bare toes, then he stands there looking up at me, with a smile on his poor one-eyed face. "So," Gary says, "how'd you—"

I put my hand up to stop him. He stops. "I want to say something, Gary, just to get things straightened out. If such a thing is possible."

He puts the toast he's holding down on his plate. He folds his arms and tips his chair back.

"What happened last night, as far as I'm concerned, was something beyond our control. It shouldn't have happened. It was . . ." I try to figure out what it was, but

181

I can't. "Well, I don't know what it was. But I want you to understand that today, this morning, right now, it doesn't mean anything. It's just something that grew out of the moonlight and the wine and the fact that we were up here alone. It's something that won't ever happen again."

He looks at me without saying anything, hard enough to make me wish he would. Then his chair tips forward onto the floor. "Okay," he says. "It didn't mean a thing."

Somehow, I'm not expecting him to go along with it so completely, and for a second it catches me off guard. I clear my throat. "I just wanted to get it out of the way, that's all. So there won't be any misunderstandings."

"No misunderstandings," he says. "None at all. And now that it's out of the way, what do you say we start over?" He smiles. " 'Morning, Mandy. Hungry?"

I nod.

"I walked up to the store this morning. Got some bread and some cereal. Milk." He picks up a box of Cheerios. "You still like these?"

I nod again, even though I haven't had them in years. I sit down. I rearrange my bowl, my spoon, my glass. I pour some Cheerios into the bowl. He pushes a banana across the table to me.

"Thank you."

"You're welcome."

I slice the banana across the top of the cereal, pour on some milk.

"The sun was out for a while, but it seems to be clouding up now," he says.

"Really?" I look out the window. "It is getting cloudy, isn't it?"

"Pretty cloudy."

I eat some Cheerios. He spreads blackberry jam on his toast.

There must be things we can talk about that have nothing to do with the fact that we made love all night, but right now I can't seem to think of any. I take another spoonful of Cheerios and drop a slice of banana on the table.

Gary pours himself a glass of orange juice. "Want some?"

"No," I say, although I do, and it makes absolutely no sense why I said I didn't.

"Toast?" he asks.

"Yes, please." I take a slice and put it on my napkin.

He chews on his toast. I pick up the banana and plop it back into the bowl.

"Ringo seems a lot better," he says. "The swelling's going down."

"That's great."

We both look at Ringo. Gary tears a piece of crust off his bread and gives it to him. I push at the bananas and Cheerios with my spoon.

"It really stinks what he's going to do," I say.

"What who's going to do?"

"Ramón. Making money off of something like that. I mean, here's a treasure people buried with their king, and all it means to Ramón is enough money to buy another Maserati."

Gary looks up from his toast. "He drives a Maserati?"

I nod.

"Do you know which model?"

I stare at him for a second. "Does it really matter?"

"I was just curious, Mandy. There aren't all that many around."

We eat in silence for a while.

"So now you're mad," he says.

"I am not mad."

"Yeah, you're mad."

"I was trying to make a point, Gary. Not have a discussion about sports cars."

"I got your point," he says. "You're full of moral outrage. A person can understand moral outrage and still be interested in a car that goes from zero to a hundred and twenty in . . . forget it. You want some coffee?"

"Please."

We both drink in silence.

When he's finished, he tips his chair back on its legs again. "Okay, this is what I think. I think you should call your answering machine and pick up your messages. Ramón's probably been trying to call you."

"And then what?"

He shrugs. "Then we play it by ear. Find out whatever we can. I mean, right now, we're free agents. Nobody knows where we are. Nobody knows where the envelope is. And one thing I do not want to do is deliver the papers to the wrong people. The bastards who tried to kill our dog, for instance."

"They seem willing to kill more than that, Gary."

I eat one more banana slice and put my spoon down. "I need to call work again. I'm going to end up using all my sick days on this thing."

"We'll walk into town when we're finished and use the phone there. And Mandy . . . ?"

I look at him.

"Even though it doesn't mean anything now, I just want you to know that it meant something then."

I look down at the Cheerios still floating in the milk.

"More toast?" he says.

I take a piece off the plate he's holding even though I haven't touched the first piece yet. "Thank you," I say.

He smiles. "You're welcome."

There are thirteen messages on my machine. Six are from Charlene. She sounds a little more frantic in every one. "Are you okay?" she keeps saying. "Where the heck are you? Amanda? Are you so sick you can't even answer the phone?" The other seven are from Ramón. In the first three he's perfectly charming. By the fourth the charm's wearing thin. He slams the receiver down on the fifth, and by the seventh he's hard to understand.

"How about this," Gary says. We're sitting at a little table Mr. Pennygreen keeps in his store in case someone needs to wait to use the phone, like us. "You call your machine and leave a message specifically for him."

"Gary, I have absolutely nothing to say to that man. Nothing civil. Nothing at all. Nothing. Period."

"Yeah, you do. Tell him to call you as soon as possible at the number on the pay phone."

"What? You want him to call me here?"

"Well, this is where we are."

It's that old feeling again. Gary's got the joystick, and I'm along for the ride. I sigh. "And then what?"

"Then when he calls, we'll set up a place to meet. To give him the key."

"We're going to give him the key?"

"Sure. I mean, we can give anyone the key. It's not going to lead him to the papers, right?"

"Right. So then why are we going to give it to him?"

"Well, we're not going to give it to him, we're just going to say we're going to give it to him. Then when we meet to do that, we tell him the key's not going to do him any good and see what happens."

"And what if what happens isn't pleasant?"

"That's why we're going to set up a meeting in a very public place. To discourage that kind of thing."

"One question," I say.

"What?"

"Why are we doing this?"

"Well, I've been thinking about that." He starts counting off on his fingers. "First of all, if Ramón trashed your house and used you to carry his illegal loot, then he deserves a considerable amount of grief. Second, if he didn't break into your house but he is a shit, then he still deserves some grief. Third, even if he is innocent on all counts, he still might be able to shed some light on who the real bad guys are." He stops for a second, but he's not finished. "Fourth," he says, "we both get to avenge our moral outrage over what happened to Ringo." He sits back.

I watch him for a moment. "Fine. Now what's the real reason?"

He watches me back. "I want to meet this guy," he says, in a certain tone of voice.

And so now I know. Even though it might be about

all those other things, it's mainly about me. And I also know that he's going to see Ramón one way or the other, and that it will probably be better for everyone if I'm there when he does.

"And where is this very public place that will discourage unpleasant behavior?" I ask.

He shrugs. "You name it."

I think about it. "How about the park?"

He frowns. "Someone got murdered there in broad daylight a couple of years ago, and no one even called the cops until it was too late."

"How about the new mall?"

He makes a face. "Maybe," he says. Gary hates malls.

Half a dozen possibilities go through my head and I reject them one by one. All except the last. "The Science Museum?" I say.

"The Science Museum." He likes it, I can tell. "Lots of guards with walkie-talkies," he says. "We could set it up for the Aviation wing. I know that place like the back of my hand. The Aviation wing of the Science Museum this afternoon at—" He looks at his watch. "—three o'clock." I tear a deposit slip out of my checkbook and write it on the back. I put the note in the middle of the table. Then I go over to the phone. I call my machine, take a deep breath, and leave a message. "Ramón, you can reach me this morning at . . ."

I go back to the table, sit down, fold my arms. Gary tips his chair back. We try hard not to look at each other. The phone rings. Gary almost falls over backward. "Christ," he says, "that was quick."

He follows me over to the booth. "Wait a second," he

says. He runs back to the table and grabs the deposit slip. "And remember," he says, handing it to me, "you don't know about the key. You have to wait for him to tell you about it."

We can't close the door with both of us inside, but since you have to yell at Mr. Pennygreen to make him hear when you're standing right next to him, it doesn't seem to make any difference.

I pick up the phone. My throat goes dry, and I don't know if anything's going to come out. "Hello?"

There's three seconds of silence. "Amanda? Is that you?"

"Charlene?"

"Amanda, what's wrong with you? Where the hell are you? How come your voice sounds funny?"

"Charlene, why are you calling me here?"

Gary groans. He hits his forehead with his palm. He walks back to the table.

"I've been calling you at home since yesterday morning. You've had me worried sick. I even went over to your place last night. No lights. No car. Where the heck are you, anyway? And how come you're leaving messages for Ramón instead of me?"

"Charlene, I'm up at the lake and I'm fine. Everything's fine. And I left the message for Ramón because I have something of his he's very anxious to get back. I was going to call you. You just didn't give me a chance."

"Amanda . . ." She has that I-know-you're-up-to-something-you're-not-telling-me-about tone in her voice. "Amanda . . . are you alone up there?"

"No. Ringo's here, too."

"I wasn't talking about Ringo."

"And Gary."

I hear her gasp. "You're kidding."

"No, Charlene. I'm not kidding. But look, I'm waiting for another call, so I have to go. I'll explain everything when I see you, I promise."

She lets out a big sigh. "And here I thought I was your best friend."

"You are. So act like one and hang up, okay?"

Gary shakes his head when I get back to the table.

"She was worried," I tell him.

"At least we know your machine works," he says.

We wait some more. I keep looking at my watch. Five minutes, ten, fifteen. Gary starts ripping matches out of the pack and making shapes on the table with them.

"I can't stand this," I say.

He looks up. "I thought I was supposed to be the impatient one."

"I'm not impatient. I'm a nervous wreck."

Mr. Pennygreen glances over at us. I smile at him. Gary starts making letters with the matches. It's a game. But since he only has enough to make three or four letters at a time, I have to remember them in my head to get the word he's spelling. He makes N O V E M, and I say "November." He makes 1 4. That was our first date. He makes C H O C C H I P S U N D A E S, which is what we used to have for dinner practically every Friday night. He makes H O W C O M E Y O U D I D N T G E T F A T with a little pointed question mark after it.

And then the phone rings.

Gary pushes the deposit slip toward me.

"If it's Charlene again," he says, "tell her I'm going to kill her."

But it isn't Charlene.

"Amaahnnda," Ramón says, "I'm so relieved. I had given up hope of ever finding you again."

"Well, actually," I say, "I've been on a sort of vacation."

"Ah, well," he says, "very good. But as I explained on your machine, when you picked up your things you may have taken something I need, without realizing it, of course. Something I stupidly put inside, of all things—" He laughs. "—the nest of crocodiles."

"Inside the nest of crocodiles?" I wanted to sound surprised, not shocked. But Gary nods at me as though I'm doing just fine.

"Did you take them?"

"Well, yes, as a matter of fact I did."

"Aahh, Amaahnda. You don't know how relieved I am to hear that. But let me explain. You know how it is, you put something in a safe place so you won't forget where it is, and the place is so safe that you forget where it is?"

We both laugh a little.

"It is a key. Inside the nest of crocodiles. A key that I need back. You've looked inside and found it, by chance?"

"No. No, I haven't."

"The problem is, I need it very soon. Today. You do have them? The nest of crocodiles?"

"Oh yes. I have them."

"But not with you on vacation, of course."

"Well, actually, yes. I do have them with me."

"Then if you could check, Amahnda, if you could open them and tell me the key is there, it would put my mind at rest."

"Well, you just hold on, Ramón, and I'll go look."

"Thank you," he says. "Thank you."

I hold the phone away from my ear.

"What are you doing?" Gary mouths at me.

"Shhh." I mouth back.

I count to twenty. Gary walks out of the booth and back again, looking exasperated.

"Ramón? I found it. The key. I have it."

"Amahnda, you have saved my life. Now, how shall we arrange for me to pick it up?"

"Well," I say, "as a matter of fact, I'm coming into the city this afternoon. To the Science Museum. Could we meet there?"

"The Science Museum? You mean on Kennedy Drive, yes?"

Gary starts mouthing "aeronautics aeronautics" at me. I turn my back on him.

"Yes, exactly. Now let's see ... where should we meet. ... I know, how about at the entrance to the aeronautics exhibit."

"Aeronautics," he says.

"At—let's say—three o'clock?"

"Three o'clock. On the dot. And Amahnda, this is so good of you. Thank you. Thank you."

"You're welcome. You're welcome." He hangs up.

"You scumbag," I say to the phone.

I turn around to see Gary's shocked expression.

"He'd already hung up," I say. "He didn't hear that last part." I place the receiver back into the cradle. "Done."

"Yesssss," he says, with a little body English. We smile at each other. "You were great. Very cool."

"I was good, wasn't I? I mean, I had my doubts at first, but hey . . ."

His smile disappears. He looks at his watch. "Three o'clock," he says. "We gotta go. But first I have to make a call."

He picks up the phone and punches in the numbers. "Hi, J.D.," he says, then pauses, "Look, J.D., it's a long story and I don't have time right now. Has anyone been hanging around there? Yeah, what kind of questions?" He nods. "That's Amanda's car. Yes, Amanda." He slips the bottom of the phone under his chin. "J.D. says hello."

"Hi, J.D.," I say loud enough so he can hear.

"Yeah, she is," Gary says. "Yeah, she is. Yeah . . ." He looks at me. "I guess you could say that." He winks at me. "Listen, J.D., I'm going to take the seaplane into Old Jefferson."

Old Jefferson's where the airfield used to be before they moved it to New Jefferson.

"Do something for me, okay? Get a car over there? No, not hers, leave that just where it is. The Jeep maybe. Have the Catman drive it over in about a half hour and tell him to wait for me, okay? Yeah, yeah, I will." He glances at me, then away. "No, that I won't." He hangs up.

"Won't what?"

"It's not nice to listen in on other people's conversations."

"Who's this Catman?"

"Our mechanic. He lives with about a hundred and thirty-five cats." He grabs my hand. "C'mon, we gotta go."

"Thanks, Mr. Pennygreen," I call on the way out.

He waves. "Nice to see you two people together again," he says.

I glance at Gary, but if he heard, he's not letting on.

The plane rises, and I watch the lake get smaller and smaller beneath us. Behind us, Ringo sighs, and I reach my hand back to pat him without looking away from the view. I catch a glimpse of the cabin's silver roof just before the trees close around it, and for a second, in spite of myself, in spite of everything my head tells me, and in spite of everything I said to Gary this morning, I wish last night wasn't last night. I wish it was tonight, and tomorrow night and the next night, and how am I supposed to handle this, anyway? How many times am I supposed to get this person out of my system in one lifetime? I decide one way to begin is by not thinking about it. I watch the gauges, the land rolling by beneath us, the sky. I think about the way he kissed the inside of my thighs, and I shiver.

"So," I say, "is this a new plane?"

He sits there frowning, as though he's thinking about it, trying to remember if the plane's new or the plane's old or maybe if we're in a plane at all.

"Gary?"

"We have to be careful, Amanda," he says. "We have to make sure we keep this thing under control."

"I know," I say. "That's exactly what I was just thinking about myself."

"Otherwise, someone could get hurt."

"And I guess we've done enough of that already, huh?"

He gives me a funny look. "So I keep trying to come up with something that'll give us the upper hand."

"Upper hand?"

"Right. Like, everybody who's ever played sports knows that you always have the advantage when you're playing your own game on your own field."

I just look at him.

"It's a question of element, Mandy. If we're out of ours, then we lose before we begin. But if we're in and *they're* out, then maybe we end up holding all the aces." He looks over at me. "Know what I mean?"

I nod my head like one of those little dogs people used to stick in the back windows of their cars.

"Take gliding, for example," he says. "If I take off out around the cliffs, it's a piece of cake. Because I know all those drafts, all those currents. It's my backyard. It's where I learned to do it in the first place. But you take someone who's never glided over that kind of geography, and they're going to piss in their pants."

"And I take it that's what you want to make Ramón do—piss in his pants."

"Ramón," he says, "or whoever it was playing kickball in your house, whoever it was who cracked Ringo on the head."

I look down and watch our shadow cross trees and fields, the roofs of houses, a four-lane highway. "Well, we only have about an hour," I say, "so besides making him wet himself, do you have any suggestions about how exactly we're going to handle this thing this afternoon?"

"Yeah, I guess we should have a couple of plans, depending on how it goes."

But before we can work much of it out, Old Jefferson comes into view.

"Make sure your belt's good and tight," he says. "This runway's probably gone all to hell."

I hold on to the edges of my seat and think about what Gary said about elements. About being in them and out of them. That's our problem, Gary's and mine. We're opposite elements. Fire and Water. Earth and Air. We come together in bursts of incredible fireworks. But for the long haul, for all that space between the noise and the dazzle, we miss, we don't connect, we read each other all wrong.

"Hold on," he says, "we're going in."

CHAPTER TWENTY

We're standing under a replica of the *Spirit of St. Louis* while a busload of eight-year-olds makes enough noise to puncture both my eardrums.

I look at my watch again.

"Don't worry," Gary says, "he'll be here. He wants his key."

On the way over here we decided on several things. We decided that we needed to be very cool about this. As though meetings like this are something we do all the time. "Ramón," I'll say, "the key won't do you any good. We have the papers. We've turned them over to Customs. The authorities know all about you, all about what you've been doing. But if you turn over the artifact, they'll let you go. This time." The part about getting the artifact was my idea. That way, I told Gary, we can see that it's returned to whoever really owns it.

"And you think he'll give it to us?" Gary asked. He snapped his fingers. "Just like that?"

"He won't have any choice," I said. "As far as he's concerned, the jig will be up."

"The jig will be up," Gary repeated. "What exactly does that mean, anyway?"

The fact that we actually have no intention of keeping Ramón out of trouble over this doesn't bother me in the least. I hope they confiscate his store, his car, his precious grandfather clock. I hope for the rest of his life he's sorry he met me.

And then I see Ramón. He comes in with a woman wearing a black long-sleeve silk dress. The way her hair's pulled back into a bun at the back of her neck makes me think of a schoolteacher or a librarian, and I wonder if he's doing the same thing to her, using her the same way he used me. I decide I'm going to warn her, tell her what a rotten sonofabitch he is. She stops just inside the entrance to the exhibit, and then she kind of leans back against the wall, and there's something about the way she does it, something about the way she pushes out one hip that makes me think, That's no schoolteacher.

Ramon looks around, takes a step in our direction. He looks thinner than I remember, and a lot less composed. His suit is wrinkled. Then he sees me. He smiles.

"Is that him?" Gary says, turning his back to Ramón. I nod.

"Remember," Gary says and bends his head toward me. "Keep it cool."

Right, I think, right. I take deep breaths. But something happens to me, seeing Ramón. Knowing what I know, and having gone through what I've gone through. Suddenly, all I can think about is how he used me, how he offered me up as a sort of sacrificial lamb, how he manipulated me with his charm, how he made love to me without really caring, how he ignored my calls until *he* needed one more thing from me. I think about my poor wrecked house. My poor wrecked dog. About sleeping with Gary last night. And how none of it would have happened, none of it, if it weren't for him.

"Amahnda . . ." he coos. He puts his arms out like he's going to hug me, *hug* me.

"You sonofabitch," I say. "You lousy bastard."

It probably would have been okay, he probably wouldn't have heard a word I said, if it hadn't been for the fact that just as I say it, there's a sudden lull in the whole museum, as though everyone in the place has stopped talking except me.

He freezes.

"Ah fuck," Gary says.

He hears Gary, too. Then everyone else in the museum starts talking again and you can't hear a thing.

Ramón spins around and starts for the entrance, but a bunch of kids playing airplane with their arms stretched out run in front of him. He tries to dodge them, but they change direction, and all of a sudden Gary's beside him, hugging him, looking for all the world like he's just found his old lost best friend, except for the fact that Ramón's right arm is bent up behind his back in what could be considered a painful position.

"Ramón," Gary says very loudly, "amigo. Let's go someplace where we can hear ourselves think, huh?"

I follow them through the crowd, wishing I were anywhere but here, wishing I'd let Ramón keep my stuff till it rotted, wishing I'd never met him in the first place.

Ramón tries to look at me over his shoulder, "So Manny got to you, huh?" he says.

I'm trying to figure out what he's talking about, when

all of a sudden Gary stops, and I walk right into his back.

"Tell her not to try anything," he says to Ramón. He hugs Ramón tighter. "Tell her."

I look over at the schoolteacher. I look at her eyes. I've seen eyes like that before. They were in a wolverine. And this wolverine is ready for something.

"You want your key, Ramón?" Gary says. "If you want your key, tell her to back off now. She puts it away and I let you go, then we talk, and then you get your key."

"Who the hell are you?" Ramón says.

"Do you want the key or not?"

Ramón looks from Gary to me, then back again. He looks at his schoolteacher with the wolverine eyes and shakes his head. She backs away, and Gary lets go of Ramón, who turns and looks at me, rubbing his arm. "Who the hell is this guy, anyway?"

"My ex-husband," I say.

"Jesus Christ." He rubs his arm some more.

Gary waits for the wolverine to go first, and the four of us walk back through the lobby, past the ticket booth, outside, and down the marble stairs. Like old friends.

Gary points to a bunch of white tables with sun umbrellas. "This looks like a good place to talk," he says.

"Why didn't we meet out here in the first place?" Ramón asks.

Gary sits down next to him. "You didn't like the exhibits?" He stares at Ramón, then he looks hard at me and I know what he's thinking. I give him a cut-it-out-and-let's-get-this-over-with look.

"So what's this about?" Ramón says. "Why did you try to break my arm in there?"

"Because you looked like you were leaving." Gary glances across at the schoolteacher. "Why was she ready to open a direct route to my spleen?"

"Because you looked like you were forcing me to leave," Ramón says.

I glance at the schoolteacher, whose hair is loose now, and she doesn't look like a schoolteacher at all anymore.

Ramón looks at me. "Amahnda," he says. Some of the old tenderness comes back into his eyes. "You didn't need to bring him. I realize I was less than gracious about getting your things back to you, but if I'd realized how upset you were ..."

"You have no idea," I say.

"Who's Manny, Ramón? And why would he need to get to anybody?" Gary says.

"No one," Ramón says. "I was momentarily confused. Do you blame me? Now, if I can have my key, I'll buy you two a carafe of wine to show there are no hard feelings, and Carla and I will be on our way."

"Is he the one who kicked his way through her house the other night?" Gary asks. "Or did you do that yourself?"

Ramón looks at us. He looks like he's heard something frightening. "Someone was in your house?" he says.

I nod.

"They took things? The television, the stereo, jewelry?"

"Nothing," I say. "Nothing was missing."

His shoulders cave a little. He looks around.

"We weren't followed, if that's what you're worried about," Gary says.

Ramón makes a noise. It's a kind of short bark that's probably supposed to be a laugh, but it doesn't sound very convincing. "Now, why would I be worried about something like that?"

Gary shrugs. "Beats me."

Ramón leans toward me across the table. "But you have the key?"

I reach into my bag and take it out, put it down in the middle of the table.

His shoulders square. He smiles. He picks it up.

"Roomy, those lockers," Gary says.

Ramón freezes.

"We'll tell you our story," Gary says, "if you'll tell us yours." And I can see he's enjoying this. Enjoying making Ramón squirm.

Ramón sets the key on the table, sits back, folds his arms. He nods at Gary. "Please, go ahead."

"First of all," Gary says, "you used Mandy to bring stuff through Customs you were too fuck-assed scared to bring yourself. Second, you got her house trashed and her dog's head fractured." He reaches over and picks up the key. "Third, you got her involved in this." He tosses it back on the table. "Fourth, Customs is all over her. And fifth, sorry amigo, but your locker's fucking empty."

It's a little like watching a cake rise and fall through the glass window in the oven door, the way Ramón puffs up, gets red, his veins pulsing blue just under the skin at his temples. Then he deflates, goes pale, his eyes saggy at the corners, everything about him sort of caved in and hollow.

The wolverine turns in her seat and looks across the street, away from Ramón, as if seeing him all defeated like this might make her want to devour him.

"Your turn," Gary says.

Ramón sighs. "One question, amigo. Who has the papers?"

"Questions later," Gary says.

He sighs again. "It was chickenshit, what she carried in. Nothing anyone would have even been detained for. Trinkets. Of value to no one but stupid tourists who will buy anything if the patina is old and the price tag is high. Fuck-assed scared? Not exactly. But cautious, yes. Very, very cautious. As you would be, too, my friend, if you'd spent three years in a Guatemalan hell they call a jail. As for your house . . ." He looks at me. "Mine, too. My clock . . ." He shakes his head. His hands are spread on the table, and then they curl up into fists. "Manny is my cousin, but even ties of blood have a breaking point. He fucked me in Guatemala. He was going to fuck me again. But this time—this time I got lucky, and I fucked him first."

He smiles for half a second. "Those papers were for him. I intercepted them. Do you know what they are worth? I paid fifty thousand dollars for them." He pauses, as though he wants to make sure the figure sinks in. "But to get them back," he says, "my cousin is going to pay much more." He glances from Gary to me. "Five hundred thousand," he says. Another pause. "And that," he says, "I will split with you."

Gary and I look at each other.

"I think what we need to do here," Gary says, "is get a little moral outrage on the table. Your turn," he says to me.

"As far as your money goes," I begin, "you can stick it up your ass."

Ramón looks as if he's been wounded.

"And as far as the papers go, they've already been turned over to Customs. The fact is, they'd be here right now carting you away if it weren't for me. I'm the one who's keeping you out of prison."

He sighs. "What do you want?"

The wolverine clears her throat and seems about to say something. Ramón looks at her. "I have no car," he says. "I have no money. I have no goods. I'll cut out my heart before I go back into a jail. Any jail. What the fuck do you want me to do?"

She turns her head and looks back at the street.

"I want the artifact. And a letter from you stating that I had nothing whatsoever to do with any of this. That anything I transported across the border, I did so unwittingly."

"The letter," he says, "I will give you right now. But how in hell am I supposed to get the goods?"

For a second no one says anything.

"You don't have the goods?" Gary asks.

Ramón shakes his head, and I can almost hear whatever chance our sorry plan had cracking into a million pieces. "Of course not," he says. "Why do you think Manny would pay half a million for the fucking papers?"

"Because Manny has the goods," Gary says.

Ramón nods.

Gary lets out a long breath. "Without the artifact," he says, "Customs will be very unhappy. They'll want somebody's ass. And it's going to have to be yours, amigo."

Ramón's hands contract into fists so tight, his fingers turn white.

"Unless," Gary says. "You can give us the artifact *and* Manny. Then Customs would have the goods and somebody else's ass."

For a second it almost looks like Ramón's going to smile, but only for a second. "How the hell am I supposed to do that?"

"You'll find out tomorrow," Gary says. "Call the same number you called today. Call at noon."

Ramón nods.

"And don't think about going anywhere," Gary adds, "because you won't get very far. And you'll get them fucking mad, besides."

"Go?" Ramón says. "With what? The g-note I have left in the bank? And in what? That piece of shit I'm driving?"

He looks toward the street, then stands up so fast, he knocks his chair over.

Gary and I follow his stare to a black Taurus disappearing down the street behind the revolving yellow lights of a tow truck.

"I tried to tell you," the woman says. "But you didn't seem interested."

The Jeep hits a rut, and I have a headache from that ride in the backseat with Ringo and the wolverine, whose real name is Carla. It makes me shiver just to think about it. The way our arms kept touching because there was no room, the way she never looked at me, not once. And here we were doing them a favor. Driving them halfway across the city so they could get their goddamn car back. Like people should know better than to park in a towaway zone in the first place.

"I wouldn't have pegged him as your type," Gary says.

"He's a complete shit."

"If he's a complete shit now, then how come he wasn't six months ago?"

"He *was*, I just didn't know it then."

"You did that all the time," he says. "You still do it. You make up your mind about something and— wham—that's it. If I'd shown up at your house six months ago and told you the guy was bad news, you'd have slammed the door in my face."

"What do you mean I did it all the time?"

"Never mind."

"Don't do this 'never mind' thing," I say. "You're trying to make a point. But as usual you won't come right out with it."

"Okay," he says, "okay. It's just like with us. One minute I was a good enough husband for you, and the next minute I wasn't. Last night I was good enough for you, and this morning it's 'forget the whole thing.' You always go to the extreme."

He takes the turn onto Old Jefferson Road way too fast, and the tires squeal. Ringo slides from one side of the backseat to the other.

"So what you're saying is it was all my fault. Because I actually began to act as though I could do something besides answer a phone and sort mail. And I shouldn't have done that. I should have said, 'Oh no, you must be wrong, designing jewelry for you would mean I might not be able to rush home and make dinner for my husband every night of the week.' And I never once thought you weren't good enough for me, Gary Basch. Never. What I thought—what you made me think—was exactly the opposite. Why would you have gone looking for someone else in the first place?"

"It always comes down to that," he yells. "Always."

I yell right back. "Oh, I'm so sorry. I'll never mention the fact that you had another woman in my bed again."

We pull up next to the plane.

"And last night *was* the biggest mistake of my life," I say.

"Yeah," he says, "I know." He says it very quietly. "You already told me."

I'm feeling like all the adrenaline in the world is boiling and bubbling just below the surface of my skin.

"Did she really have a knife?" I ask.

"A stiletto."

"It all happened so fast." I look at him. "You could have gotten hurt."

"But I didn't," he says.

I undo my seat belt. He undoes his.

"Damn, it's hot in here," he says. He opens his door so Ringo can squeeze out.

"We'll have to keep it away from Ringo, you know, if we get it."

"Get what?"

"The artifact, 'the goods' you and Ramón were talking about."

"That was his word," Gary says. "I was just going along. And why do we have to keep it away from Ringo?"

"Because it might give him ideas."

"The two dogs," he says.

"You guessed it."

"I suppose it might give anyone ideas." He grins. "Maybe that's why the Mayans kept it around in the first place."

Somewhere out on the road there's a noise like a backfire, and we both turn to look out the back window at the same time.

"Guess we're a little jumpy," Gary says.

All I can think about is that our knees are touching down near the gear shift. A sudden cool breeze stirs through the open windows.

He pushes a strand of hair off my cheek.

I turn my head and brush his fingers with my lips.

In seconds we're in each other's arms.

CHAPTER
TWENTY-ONE

"The shift's sticking me in the kidney," he says.

"My leg's asleep."

We smile at each other.

"What's with us?" he says.

I shake my head. "I don't know."

I look up through the windshield. It's dark now. I slap a mosquito away.

"With all the skin in this front seat," Gary says, "he'll think he's died and gone to heaven."

He rubs his hand up and down my arm.

"I like that," I say.

"It's about the only part of me I can move."

We snuggle up even closer. Gary starts to laugh and breaks the mood.

"Did you see the look on his face when I told him the locker was empty?"

"Can you believe she just sat there and watched their car get towed?"

We're giddy, we're high. And all around us the stars are coming out.

Gary bends down and kisses my chin, my throat, my

breasts, my belly. "You," he says, "are all I want." He kisses me on the nose, then he pushes himself up.

I reach up and grab his hair and pull him back down on top of me. There's the sound of his rib cracking into the shift.

He makes a face. "You know what I think?" he asks. "I think it'd be better at the cabin."

"Better at the cabin. Right."

We grab our clothes and run naked to the plane, and Ringo races after us. Gary lifts him over the back of the seats. We throw our clothes on top of him and climb in. Ringo starts pawing the clothes into a heap, then he lies down on top of them and sighs like now he has everything in the world he could possibly need to make him happy.

"We're out of here," Gary says, and speeds down the runway.

A thin rim of light, sinking into black, is still visible along the horizon. It's such a kick flying naked, feeling like you're doing what you're not supposed to do, could never imagine doing. And the funny thing is, you don't even care.

Gary fiddles with something on the cockpit ceiling and his arm brushes my breast. My nipples go hard. It's like I'm all craving. All empty and waiting to be filled. I stare at the tops of our legs in the green light from the gauges, and it feels like it takes forever before Gary finally says, "Okay, hold on, we're going in."

We land and tie the plane to the dock. We start toward the cabin, but don't make it. We pull each other down on the grass beside the beach and slide into it, slow this time, with room to stretch and roll. Later, he takes my hand and we walk into the lake.

"Do you still eat toasted peanut butter and jelly sandwiches?" he asks.

"Yeah, once in a while." A teeny wisp of a blue cloud floats in front of the moon. "Why?"

"I just wanted to know, that's all."

"Do you still sleep with the pillow over your face?"

" 'Fraid so."

We float in the moonlight. Then he turns over and I feel his hand running up my leg. "Let's go inside," he whispers in my ear.

We make love on the floor in the living room. We make love in the bed.

"We can't keep doing this," he says. "*I* can't keep doing this."

"But we have four years to make up for," I tell him.

"We may have to consider writing off some of it."

Gary rolls over and watches me. Moonlight from the window bathes the two of us.

"I have to know something," he says.

"What?"

"I have to know if tomorrow morning you're going to tell me it was all a mistake again. That it didn't mean a thing."

"No." I say softly.

"You're sure?"

"It's not a mistake. I know it." I turn to face him. "I had this . . . thing for you, hard, with sharp edges pressing against me. But I don't feel it anymore. It's gone."

"You said that the other day after you knocked me off the dock, too, but then it seemed to come back."

"This is different, Gary. Really. It's not coming back."

He gives me a look like he's not convinced, but maybe he's willing to take the risk.

"And it does mean something," I say. "Last night meant something, too. I just didn't want to admit it."

"What did it mean? What does it mean?"

I think about it. "I don't know yet."

"You don't know yet?"

"It's happening too fast. What's it mean to you?"

He doesn't answer right away. "I guess I don't know yet, either."

"See?"

"Well, it might mean we could start over. Get back together."

"Maybe. Maybe that's what it means."

Neither of us says anything for a while.

"Amanda?"

He hardly ever calls me Amanda.

"I love you," he says.

I stare at him. That's another thing he's hardly ever said. "I wuv you," he's said that. And "Me, too," when I've said it to him first. But right now, the way he's said it, sounds like the first time. His eyes are full of what he's feeling. He means it.

"What's the plan?"

The "plan" seems to be the only thing Gary can talk about since we woke up. I unwrap the towel from my head and rub some of the water out of my hair. "We don't need a plan," I tell him, "we need to get out of this while we still can, Gary. I don't want to sit across a table from Ramón again. It's crazy." I lean toward him a little. "And in case you've forgotten, it's dangerous."

"Carla could be dangerous," he says, "but your friend, Ramón, Mandy . . ." He shakes his head.

"I don't want to talk about this on an empty stomach," I say. "Go take a shower. I'll make coffee."

He rolls over and looks at the clock. "We have two hours," he says. "Two hours."

I take a pair of ripped jeans and a white shirt all covered with black paint out of the closet. They're the only clothes in there.

"We've got to have this guy Manny at such a disadvantage that he can't do anything but what we want," he says. "How the hell are we supposed to do that?" He gets up and goes into the bathroom. The shower goes on.

I start to get dressed. "You know what I think," I say. "I think this is all about you, Gary. You and your ego. I think you're just trying to show me you're better than Ramón." I zip up my jeans, smile, and add, "Which, actually, you don't have to worry about. Because you are."

"Huh?" he says from the shower. "I can't hear you."

"Even if we get Manny," I say, raising my voice, "how are we supposed to get the dogs, too? I mean, chances are he doesn't carry them around with him wherever he goes."

I hear him drop the shampoo. "Shit," he says.

I comb my hair and step into my sandals.

"How do you get somebody to show you something he doesn't want anybody to see?" he says. "And then get him to give it to you without having to break his arms and legs?"

I take a towel off a shelf and carry it into the bathroom. Ringo's already there, waiting for Gary. His bad eye is starting to open. He's almost beginning to look normal. "I suppose it hasn't occurred to you that maybe he could break yours first?"

"It's occurred."

I clear the steam off the mirror and look at myself. The person in the mirror smiles. She looks like someone who's pretty close to being all filled up, but not quite. "Manny wants to sell it, right?" I say. "So doesn't someone who wants to buy something have to see it first?" I walk over to the window, throw it open, and look out at the dock. The plane's sitting there, white and shiny in the slanted morning sun. I think about last night, and how we did it everywhere but in the air. I decide I want to do it in the air.

"Gary?"

"Yeah?"

"You have an autopilot on the plane, don't you?"

"Why?"

I think about the last two days. I think about the way I felt walking into my ruined house. I think about Mama telling me to hold on to him this time. I think about Gary grabbing Ramón in the museum, right there under the *Spirit of St. Louis*. I think about elements, and being in and out of them. I think about whether or not the FAA has rules about screwing in the cockpit.

"I think we should do it in the air," I say.

The shower goes off. The curtain slides open.

"What did you say?"

"I said, I think we should do it in the air."

"Do it in the air?" He says it slow, like he's tasting every letter. Then he smiles and wraps his big wet self around me. "We're going to fucking do it in the air."

"Actually," I say, "I was thinking that, too."

He frowns. "Huh?"

"Never mind." I take his towel and drape it over his head.

"But how exactly," he says, "are we going to do it in the air."

"Don't ask me," I say, walking out of the bathroom. "It's time for *you* to come up with some of the answers."

I plug in the coffeemaker, pour two bowls of cereal. Ringo puts one paw on my leg. I pour some in his bowl, too.

"You think Ramón's ever jumped out of a plane?" Gary sits down at the table and starts buttoning his shirt.

"No. Why?"

"Because I think he's going to take his first jump real soon."

I pick up the orange juice, put it down again. "What, exactly, is your idea?"

"I'm not sure yet," he says, "but it's coming." He pours milk on his cereal. "Jeez, I'm starving." He looks at me. He grins. "That's your fault."

"What if he won't do it?"

"Oh, he'll do it."

"You know, Gary, not everybody thinks jumping out of an airplane at six thousand feet is a religious experience."

"He'll do it," he says again.

"How can you be so sure?"

"Machismo," he says. "It's in his genes. He won't even have a choice."

I start to protest. To tell him that I want it all to stop now. No more Ramón. No more plan. But then it hits me that he's right about Ramón. Right about the fact that he's not really dangerous. Right about the fact that he'll jump no matter how scared he is.

I watch Gary eat three bowls of cereal and several pieces of toast. There are certain parts of him—his shoulders, his jaw, his hands—that make me hot just looking at them.

"Gary?"

"Mmm?"

"You *do* have autopilot, right?"

"Sure." He empties his third glass of orange juice. He asks again. "Why?"

I shrug. I smile. "No reason. I was just wondering, that's all."

We arrive at Mr. Pennygreen's store early, a little after eleven-thirty, because I want to call Charlene just to check in with her and let her know I'm taking the whole week off, that I won't see her for a few days. To tell her not to worry, if I can sound convincing about that.

"Amanda?" she says. "I've been waiting and waiting for you to call. What on earth is going on there? Hold on."

Talking to Charlene at work is full of breaks in the

conversation. She has something like fifteen lines, and she handles them all herself.

"Are you still at the lake?" She's back. "And what the heck are you doing there? Why are you being so damn mysterious?"

"Yes, I'm still at the lake," I say, "and I don't mean to be mysterious. I'm just trying to work something out, Char. Something I wasn't expecting to *have* to work out."

"It's Gary, isn't it?" she says. "Hold on." I start counting and get as far as six. "Isn't it?" she says.

"Yes."

"You're getting back together, aren't you? Hold on."

"Char," I say when she clicks back on the line, "I can't keep talking. I have to go. I just wanted you to know everything's okay, and I'll see you as soon as I can. I'll explain everything then, all right?"

"I guess."

" 'Bye."

"Guess it's tough luck for Mr. Huntington, then."

I press the phone back against my ear. "What?"

"I said, I guess it's tough luck for Mr. Huntington."

"Who's Mr. Huntington?"

"*Philip* Huntington? You don't remember him? Oh, Amanda, guess Gary's blown your immediate past right out of existence, huh?"

"Char, what in heck are you talking about?"

"The guy on the train. The guy you talked to the day you lost your sketchbook. You told me he was nice. You didn't tell me he was cute, too."

"Huntington? That was his stop, Char, not his name."

"Well, maybe you got the stop mixed up with the

name. Anyway, he was here this morning, asking about you. He had your sketch pad. He wanted to give it back to you, but you weren't at work. So he gave it to me."

"He gave it to you? Wait a minute. Why did he give it to you? You don't even work on my floor. How did he find out I even knew you? Charlene, he doesn't know where I work. He doesn't even know my last name."

There's a silence on her side of the line. Then, "Why are you asking me all these questions? How am I supposed to know how he found you or how he found me? He had your sketchbook, didn't he? Isn't your name in it? Maybe they told him downstairs we're friends, and he wanted to find out a few things about you from someone who knew you. Or maybe he's a spy, just like your boss is so afraid of. Jeez, Amanda, you're beginning to sound paranoid. Maybe he's smitten. Though I guess that doesn't mean much now."

"What did he want to know about me?"

"Hold on," she says, "I'm lit up like a Christmas tree."

I look at my watch. Gary's starting to give me dark looks from his seat at the table. C'mon c'mon c'mon, I chant inside my head.

"So where were we?" she says.

"I was asking you what he wanted to know about me."

"Like maybe you're still interested?"

"Tell me, Char. Just tell me."

"You don't sound like yourself," she says. "You sound terminally serious."

I sigh into the phone.

"Okay. He wanted to know what your favorite flowers were, so he could send you some, since you were sick. And he seemed so concerned about you, that it didn't feel right to leave him worrying like that, so I told him I didn't think you really were that sick. But he wanted to know where he could send you flowers, and I told him where you lived, but he said he'd tried calling you there and you were never home."

My lips start to tingle. "What else did you tell him?"

"Oh c'mon," she says, "I'm not that dumb. I knew you were up there with Gary. You think I'm going to send another man up there?"

"So you didn't tell him where I am then, right?"

"Well, no. I mean, I told him you had a place at Coventry Lake, 'cause he asked me what kind of things you like to do, where you like to go. But I didn't tell him that's where you were now."

Gary gets up and comes over to the booth. He takes one look at my face and mouths, What's wrong?

"Is that it, Char? Is that everything you told him?"

"Yes. Why are you making me feel so guilty about this, Amanda? You told me yourself he was a nice guy."

"Right. Well, it was a five-minute ride, Char. People have fooled me for a lot longer than that." Gary gives me a frantic c'mon-get-off-the-damn-phone look. "Char, I gotta go. Look, don't say anything about me to anyone until we can talk again, okay? And if Mr. Huntington comes back, tell him I've gone to Brazil and I'll be there indefinitely. Char, I'm hanging up. Don't worry. I'll see you in a few days. Promise."

"What the hell was that all about?" Gary asks as soon as the receiver's back in its cradle.

"Maybe nothing . . . or something. I don't know if I can tell the difference anymore." And then the phone rings and we both jump.

"Oh God, it's Ramón." I stare at the phone. It was all in my head ten minutes ago, everything I was supposed to say. And now it's gone. I look at Gary. "I can't remember. What am I supposed to say?"

He hands me a sheet of yellow lined paper. "That's why we wrote it down. Now pick up the phone and say hello before he gets nervous and hangs up."

"Amahnda," Ramón says. "You said to call at noon. It is noon."

"Just listen, Ramón. No questions." And so I begin telling him Gary's plan.

Joe's coming in just as we're leaving the store. He has a smear of engine grease across his forehead, and he's carrying a can of Coke. He gives Gary's arm a fake punch and nods his head at me. "Get your van back from that redheaded girl in one piece?" he asks.

"Oh yeah," Gary says. "Probably the last thing she'll ever give me, though."

Joe laughs. "Way she peeled outta the garage that morning, I figured it might be."

"That's something I wanted to talk to you about, Joe," Gary says. "About your bill. There was only a small charge for parts. No labor."

Joe laughs again. "All I did was replace a hose," he says. "Besides, that's policy for bikers."

"Yeah, but I'm an ex-biker."

"Nah, no such thing."

They shake hands, and we start to walk away.

"Anyway," Joe says, "you stay away from those red-heads. Tempers match their hair." He looks at me and winks. "Stick with brunettes."

"We'll see," Gary says. "Maybe you're right."

"Maybe?" I say, when we're passing the post office.

"Sure, if you're lucky."

I give him a shove, and he takes off ahead of me. Finally, he slows down so I can catch up. "Someone was asking Charlene about me," I say when I catch my breath.

"Who?"

"A guy I met on the train last Friday. He found my sketchbook and wanted to return it."

"So?"

"I only told him my first name, Gary. But he told Charlene he'd tried to call me at home and I was never there. And then he found out where I worked. He even found out Charlene was my friend."

"Isn't your name and address on the sketchbook? Your business address?"

"That's what Charlene asked. No, nothing."

We walk along in silence, and the sun-slanted green woods begin to close in on either side of us and start to feel different. Dark and ominous.

"She told him something else." I can feel him looking at me, waiting. "She told him I had a place on Coventry Lake."

He doesn't say anything, he just starts walking faster.

We're at the last bend before the cabin when we hear a car coming up the road behind us. It's not something I can ever remember doing in my life, hiding from an oncoming car, but we don't even have to discuss it. We just get off the road and crouch behind the low branches of a giant spruce, as though it's a perfectly normal thing to do.

I can hear my heart pounding in my ears, and then an old beat-up truck passes us. "Joe," Gary says.

We catch up with him as he's coming back down the porch steps. Inside the cabin, Ringo's barking and jumping against the door, as though he's back to his old grumpy self. Joe looks at us and frowns. "How'd I miss you? You go through the woods?"

"Yeah," Gary says, "we did."

He looks at our shoes, then he scratches his head. "Ten minutes after you left, there were a couple a fellas come in asking about you." He looks at me. "About you. About your place and where they might find it. Said they were supposed to look it over and give you an estimate on some work you're thinking of doing to it. Said they lost the directions. That so?"

"No." My voice comes out sounding like a door with a rusty hinge. I shake my head.

"Didn't think so." He looks at Gary. "You spend a couple of years locked up with those guys, and you get so you can tell 'em even when they're wearing nice suits."

"So they're on their way?" Gary says.

Joe shakes his head. "You know Pennygreen, deaf as a tree. They were having trouble communicating, so I stepped in and told 'em where I thought they could find you. I sent them over the north side of the lake. But eventually they'll work their way back around."

For a while no one says anything. Then Gary clears his throat. "It's a complicated thing to explain, Joe."

"I didn't come here for no explanations," Joe says. "I came here to tell you to get the hell out." He looks around the yard. "Where's your car, anyway? You walk here?"

"Flew," Gary says. "It's on the lake."

"No kidding? You know, I'd like to try that myself sometime."

"You name it, Joe," Gary says, "you got it."

Joe starts back toward his truck, then he turns around. "Those guys," he says. "There was somethin' about them. I'd watch my ass real good."

In ten minutes we're lifting off the lake.

"So much for being free agents," Gary says. He flips some switches. "She ever have her nose fixed, by the way?"

"Charlene? No. She just talks about it."

"Well, tell her not to bother," he says. "Because the next time I see her, I'm going to fix it for her."

CHAPTER TWENTY-TWO

Ramón woke up feeling like he'd drunk three bottles of cheap wine or run into a stone wall at sixty miles an hour.

It was the gods. They were out to get him. Always ready to stick out a giant goddamn hand and stop him just when he reached for the golden ring.

He'd dreamed of stepping out of the plane, and realizing, at that moment when he stepped into nothing but air, that the pack on his chest wasn't the parachute, that the parachute was still in the plane. The pack on his chest was stuffed with half a million dollars in one-dollar bills, money that after everything he'd gone through, he was never going to get to spend.

He sat up and rubbed his eyes. The dream, his mother would say, was an *agüero*, an omen, that this thing was going to end badly. But then he didn't need a dream to tell him that.

In exchange for escaping prosecution, he would give up everything. The money Manny owed him, the Maserati he would never redeem, even the shit-assed store that Manny had never got around to putting in his name. And Carla, he'd lose her, too. Her long legs, her brown-tipped breasts, her inexhaustible passion. She'd take her expensive tastes, which he'd no longer be able to fill, and move on.

He looked around. The only good thing was that he'd never have to see this fucking motel room again.

And sure, Manny would join him in his misery for once. Manny in pain. That, he had to admit, even under these circumstances, was sweet, very sweet. Manny's chip finally coming to rest in the square marked Loser.

He heard Carla in the bathroom. She hadn't said a word when he told her the plan. He hadn't even been sure she was listening.

He got up and walked around, went over to the front door and opened it, took deep breaths of the evening air. Back in the bedroom, he sat down on the bed and picked up the phone.

"Primo," he said, when Manny answered. *"Buenas noches."*

Manny growled.

"Now is that the way to greet someone bringing you good news?"

"What the hell do you want? You can't wait until tomorrow? You have to damage this day for me as well?"

"Chill, Manny, chill. And listen very closely. I have a buyer for our item. A buyer, Manny."

"What are you talking about?"

"Hey, amigo, what do you think I do all day, lie around watching TV? I'm a businessman. I work. I find opportunities."

"The only opportunities you find, shithead, are on my back."

He wanted to take the phone and slam it down. But

unless it was in the middle of Manny's fat, ugly face, what good would it do? He took a deep breath. "Like I said, primo, I have a buyer for our property. You want to listen or not?"

There was silence. He decided to take it for assent.

"He's a collector. He collects any way he has to. He has enough money to buy the whole fucking Yucatán peninsula."

"How do you know about the Yucatán peninsula?"

"I can read, primo. The papers are in my hands, remember? You think I wouldn't check the goods out? You think I'd put myself on the line for a business deal of no consequence?"

"How do you know who he is? What if he's a *rata*?"

"He's no rat. You think I'm stupid enough to involve someone who will put me back in some stinking cell?"

"Tell him to call me." Manny didn't sound convinced.

"Oh no. This one we're in on together, remember, cousin? On this one, *I* make the deal. So listen very carefully. Tomorrow, you will drive to the airport. You will look for runway D-5. There, the buyer and I will be waiting for you. He wants to see the piece. This man is very rich, but very eccentric. He deals only in the air."

"What the hell are you saying?"

"I'm saying he will only look at the object in the air. His plane will be waiting for us. So this is the way it will go, primo. You and I and the buyer will take off. Once we're in the air, you and I will make our exchange. Then you and the buyer will conduct your business. What happens after that is between you and him."

"Jesus Christ!"

Ramón waited. The only obstacle could be if Manny already had another buyer. But this was big and not something he'd easily unload. Ramón silently prayed he'd take the bait.

"I hate flying."

"So take a pill. But be there at three o'clock. And Manny? Your part of the deal comes only after our part of the deal. Is that clear?"

"It is, you sonofabitch."

"Nobody said you had to like it, primo. Then we see you tomorrow?"

"Tomorrow." The line went dead.

Ramón sat there, staring at the phone, totally drained. He turned only when he heard the bathroom door open. Then Carla's hand was on his shoulder. Her nails trailed up and down his arm.

"Not now," he said.

How could he tell her how he felt? Would she understand his nightmare, his fear of standing at the open door of that fucking plane, knowing he had no choice but to step out into the arms of doom? And that gringo daredevil who was calling the shots. He talked about the jump as if it were a step into the arms of a lover, instead of the arms of death. It made it worse, because the gringo knew his fear and pretended to ignore it. So, on top of everything else, I am a coward, Ramón thought. He ticked his list of failings off one by one in his head. A pauper. A coward. A puppet, with someone's fist up his ass directing all his movements.

He shook his head. "Tonight," he said, "I just haven't got it."

She lifted one leg up and straddled him, kneeling on

the bed. She was cool and fresh smelling from the shower. Wearing nothing, beautiful.

"Then I'll have to help you get it back," she said.

Carla pulled the sheet down off him. He lay back and let her begin her particular magic. It would work; it was already starting to. And he would pay particular attention this time, try to store the intensity, memorize the taste and the feel and the smell of her. Because he knew what this was going to be. The end. The closing performance after a long, sweet run. The good-bye fuck. Ramón was surprised to realize how much he'd miss her.

CHAPTER TWENTY-THREE

Ringo's lying in the back seat of the Jeep letting out a growl every few seconds. It doesn't seem to bother Carla, but it's driving me crazy. She seems oblivious to the fact Ringo hates her. When she came out of the ladies' room at the Exxon station, I almost dislocated a shoulder trying to keep him from diving at her.

I glance sideways at her manicured nails. Blood-red. Like talons. She's a hard person to think warm thoughts about.

And then there's Ringo, acting mean and edgy ever since we moved into the Catman's trailer. Gary says it's the cats. "You live in a place this size with thirty cats, it's going to take a long time for the smell to go away."

I don't like living in it either, even if it is only for two nights. But I don't think it's the trailer that's Ringo's problem. I think it's something else. I think what happened to him has twisted his personality a few notches toward bitter.

Carla stretches her legs, and I flinch a little, which makes us swerve slightly. The car beside us honks.

"Watch it," she says. "I'm not doing this so I can get killed in a fucking accident."

I glance at her long enough to let her know I'm not totally intimidated. Then I look back at the road.

"We should go over what we have to do," I say.

"I know what I have to do," she says.

"Then it's time for a refresher course. First, I have to stop and pick up something in Dayville. Then we get to the airport by one and make our way to the jump site." I reach inside my jacket pocket. "Here are your directions." I hold the paper out to her. "Unless you've already *guessed* where you're supposed to meet him?" She takes it out of my hand and reads it.

Neither of us says anything else until we pull up in front of Dayville Manor.

I turn off the engine and put the keys in my pocket. "I'll be ten minutes at most." But Carla doesn't even look my way. "You know," I go on, "I can think of other places I'd rather be, too." I look at Ringo. "You be good."

I ring Mama's bell, knock on the door, then I use my key. "Mama? It's me. Amanda." I hear a noise in the kitchen. "Mama, it's me." I turn the corner from the living room onto the yellow tile floor and stop short. A man is sitting at her kitchen table.

"Quite the cat-and-mouse game you've been playing with us, Amanda Basch. Welcome to the trap."

Philip Huntington. Somehow he doesn't seem anywhere near as nice as he did on the train. "Where's my mother? Where's her nurse?"

"A very confused woman, your mother. Can't seem to come up with a straight answer to save her life. How can you stand it?" He shakes his head. "The nurse— Rose, isn't it?—is resting comfortably. And will continue to do so for several more hours. Mother had a small accident, I'm afraid."

I hear him, but it's like he's talking in slow motion. Or like I'm hearing in slow motion. "Where is she?"

"At the hospital. It was just a little fall. Did you know that old people fall because their bones break, rather than the other way around?"

I start to back away.

"Don't," he says. "I do have a gun, and it does have a silencer, but I'd rather not have to use it yet." He stands up. "In fact, I'd rather not have to use it at all."

"I want to see my mother. I want to know if she's all right."

"By all means, call the hospital. They've been trying to call you all day, I'm sure. But you've been very very difficult to find." He motions to the phone.

I check the list of programmed emergency numbers on the phone and wait for the autodial.

"I want to check on an admission," I say. "A Mrs. Sadie O'Toole. She may have been brought in as an emergency this morning. I'm her daughter." I hold my breath while I wait.

"Ms. O'Toole?"

"Yes."

"I'm Dr. Pearce. I admitted your mother."

"Is she all right?"

"She's comfortable now. It appears she fell and broke her hip."

The front door opens. Carla comes through first, then a man I've never seen before. He's wearing a Dayville Manor custodian coverall.

"Oh God," I say. "How did it happen?"

"She was very unclear about that. She kept saying the man next door pushed her, but, of course, with her condition, it's difficult to know."

I spin around and face Huntington. More than anything, I want to take that smug smile off his face and choke him with it.

"She's asleep, Ms. O'Toole. She will be for a while. We've been trying to reach you."

"I was away. I just got back. Tell her I'll be there as soon as I can."

Huntington's eyebrows go up, as though he's doubtful of what I've just said.

"Now," Huntington says when I hang up, "let's get this over with as quickly and sensibly as we can." He looks over at Carla.

She pulls her elbow out of the custodian's grip and stares at Huntington with her piercing eyes. "Who the fuck are you?"

"Amazing," he says. "Both of you so elusive. And both of you right here." He takes a spoon out of a coffee mug in front of him and taps it on the table. "You see, I have a boss. And right now, he's a very unhappy man." He stops tapping and looks at me. "A casualty was left in a public place." He taps the spoon once. "He hates that sort of display. Though I did try to explain how we couldn't let anyone hurt you before we even had a chance to talk."

My lips start to tingle, and I feel my center of gravity shift. Don't faint, don't faint, I keep yelling inside my head.

"And then we wasted all that time tracking the UPS truck." He smiles. "Though we did wonder for a while why you were making such frequent stops. Ultimately, however, your girlfriend was most helpful. A little too voluble for your liking, I'm sure—especially the part about the terrible stress you've been under because of your mother. That, she volunteered with no prompting whatsoever." He taps the spoon one more time. "Such a lovely smile, a lovely girl. Your cabin, by the way, is a little gem. It will take you a while to put it back together I fear."

If Charlene were here, I think, I'd kill her.

He drops the spoon back into the mug. The sound rings in my ears. "So then," he says, "enough time wasted. Where is it, ladies?"

"Did you check your asshole?" Carla says.

Huntington's eyes turn black, his jaw goes rigid. All of a sudden the air is too thin to breathe. The walls start to recede.

"I'm going to be sick," I say.

"Shut up!" he yells.

I cover my mouth with my hand. My stomach convulses.

"Sonofabitch, get her out of here!" Huntington says to his man.

I stumble into the bathroom, kneel in front of the toilet, lose it.

"Oh, Christ," the custodian mumbles as he goes out into the hall. I retch again. Then I see a bowling ball swimming in my tears. My father's old bowling ball. It's sitting right next to the toilet, a swirl of black and gray, with sparks of red glitter. Out of the corner of my eye I can see the custodian's heels facing me in the hallway. I slip my fingers into the holes, make one more disgusting noise, and stand up as fast as my shaky knees will let me. It's the same arm I used to hold Ringo back in the Jeep, and when I swing the ball, my shoulder hurts like hell. But the custodian goes down on the rug.

I stand there, holding the ball, afraid to move, afraid to breathe. I hear Huntington's voice droning in the kitchen. Outside, a lawn mower buzzes. Without turning around, I feel for the shelves, push my free hand under the bottom towel. A corner of the envelope slices under my fingernail and I pull my hand away fast. The bowling ball falls on the floor.

"Sonofabitch," Huntington says from the doorway. He looks from the custodian crumpled at his feet to me. He pulls a gun out from under his jacket and shoves Carla toward the living room. "Both of you in here. Now." He backs away as I step over the custodian.

He motions me toward the living room. "We'll just take a ride to a place where things are a little more under control." Then there's a crash from the bedroom, and he spins around just in time to catch a snarling mass of dog right in the chest. They go down on the floor, and the gun goes off twice. It seems to last forever, Ringo with Huntington's throat between his jaws, Huntington's head flopping from side to side, me yelling.

Finally, I pull Ringo off. I look at Huntington. "Did Ringo kill him?"

"Maybe," Carla says. "But I think the fucker died when he shot himself. C'mon, we have to get out of here."

She's pulling me through the front door, but I shake her off. "I have to get something." I turn back, avoid looking at Huntington, step over the custodian, pull the envelope out from under the towels.

Outside, Carla spots a delivery man parked across the street.

"Oh shit," she says.

"What's happening over there?" he yells.

"Break-in," I yell back. "Call the police."

"Don't say that," Carla hisses.

"Already on the way," he replies, waving his cellular in the air.

"Great." Carla puts out her hand. "Keys," she says. I hand them to her. "Now get in. And don't let that dog of yours get any blood on me."

We're three blocks away when two cruisers pass us with their sirens blaring.

"Where the hell did that bowling ball come from?"

All of a sudden my shoulder starts to hurt. I rub it. "It was my father's," I say. I feel her looking at me. "Where are we going?"

"To the fucking airport," she says. "That was next, after your 'no more than ten minutes' at Dayville Manor, right? Christ, I can hardly wait to see what's waiting for us there."

"We can't go to the airport," I say. "We have to go to the hospital."

"What the fuck for?"

"My mother's there with a broken hip. And it's all my fault."

"You're fucking insane. Why do you think they put her there in the first place? Can't you figure it out? They're waiting for you there, too."

"Look," I say, "my mother's seventy-eight years old.

Half the time she acts like she's a baby. She's scared. She's hurt. She needs me. Didn't you ever have a mother?"

She looks at her watch. "We're supposed to be at the airport at one. We're already late."

"They don't take off until three. Two hours early was just Gary being paranoid."

She pulls over and makes a U-turn. "For your information," she says through clenched teeth, "I do have a mother."

I turn around and look at Ringo. He's licking his paws. He glances up at me, then starts licking again, and I wonder what happens to a dog once they've had the taste of blood. He glances at me again, and I look away, remembering that's something you only have to worry about with lions.

CHAPTER
TWENTY-FOUR

"Look," Carla says when we're parked in the hospital garage. "This is my gig. You do what I say now. Follow me."

"What can possibly happen?" I ask. "It's a hospital. It's full of people. How can they do anything in a hospital full of people?"

"You don't know a thing, do you?" She leans toward me a little, and Ringo growls deep in his throat from the backseat. "If it hadn't been for that bowling ball, we'd probably both be dead. Dead," she says again, "or wishing we were. And it doesn't matter to them where you are. In church. In bed. Or in the middle of a fucking hospital. Now let's go before I change my mind. And remember, you do whatever I tell you to do."

Halfway to the reception desk, she hisses, "What's your mother's name?"

"Sadie O'Toole."

She gets an upset look on her face and breaks into a trot. "I'm Amanda O'Toole," she half yells at the woman behind the desk. "My mother Sadie was brought in this morning with a broken hip. What room is she in?"

"Room 432," the woman says, "and she's in satisfactory condition, so do try and be calm."

Carla grabs my hand and pulls me toward the elevator. We ride up in silence with a priest and a man holding a bunch of balloons. At the nurse's station Carla taps my keys on the counter. Two nurses look up. "I'm Amanda O'Toole," she says. "I'm here with my friend to see my mother in 432."

They both nod. "Six rooms down, on the left," one of them says, pointing.

The door to 432 is closed. The hallway's empty. "Don't say a word," she says, then she pushes the door open. The first thing she does is go over to the windows and close the blinds.

I head for the bed closest to the door. It's empty. I bang into the foot of the bed, trying to get around it.

Carla opens the bathroom door, and a shaft of light falls across the second bed. Mama's eyes are closed, and she looks about half the size I remember.

"Get in the bathroom," she says, "and stay there until I tell you to come out."

I look at Mama. I hesitate.

"Now," she hisses.

Inside the bathroom I turn off the light and leave the door open just a crack. I watch Carla open her bag and take something out, watch her position herself next to Mama, with her back to the door.

"Ma?" she says. "Ma, can you hear me?"

Mama exhales a deep breath. She stirs. "Who the fuck are you?" she says.

Then the door opens. A doctor stands framed in bright light for a moment, and then he steps inside. The

door closes, the light disappears, and for a few seconds
I can't see a thing.

"Mrs. Basch?" he says.

"Yes," Carla answers. "I'm Mrs. Basch."

I hear his footsteps on the tile, then I hear a noise like
the last bit of air puffing out of a balloon, and a thud.
I open the door.

"I told you to stay in there."

I look at the body on the floor. "Oh my God." I grab
onto the bed rail. "You killed a doctor, for Christ's
sake."

"I didn't kill anyone," she says. She tosses her bag
on the empty bed and bends down, lifts him under the
arms. "Don't just stand there, help me." We drag him
across the tile into the bathroom. "And this," she says,
"is no fucking doctor."

"You don't know that!"

She shoves the door shut against him. Goes over to
the windows and opens the blinds. We stand there
blinking at each other.

"Think about it," she says. "What name did I give to
the receptionist? What name did I give to the nurse out
there? What did he call me when he walked in?"

Mama moans. "Mama?" I take her hand. It's cold,
and I hold it between both of mine to warm it. "It's me,
Mama. Amanda. I'm so sorry you got hurt."

She opens her eyes. She looks from me to Carla and
back again. "Amanda," she says, "now you make sure
you remember to water my plants till I get home." Then
she closes her eyes and goes back to sleep.

                        * * *

"He's a maniac," I say. "He's willing to do anything. And Gary's going to be alone with him in a goddamn plane."

Carla shifts the Jeep into fifth and looks at me as though she doesn't know what I'm talking about.

"Everything that's happened," I say. "Accidents, guns, dead people, wrecked houses."

"Yeah?" she says. "You think you're talking about Manny?" She laughs, but there's nothing funny about it. "Manny's a schmuck." Then she whips off the highway one exit before the airport.

"What are you doing?" I look at my watch. "We've got less than half an hour before they take off."

She doesn't answer. She drives five minutes down the road and pulls into a Ryder rental.

"What are we doing here?"

"This is where I get out," she says. "I have no reason to go to the airport. You're the one who has to get that envelope there by three." She glances at my bag. The top of the manila envelope's just visible. She gets out and slams the door. She starts to leave, stops, turns around again. She fishes something out of her bag. "Here," she says. "Maybe you want these." She tosses a package on the seat. Then she walks away.

CHAPTER TWENTY-FIVE

Gary tells himself it was the right decision to use National Airport to fly out of today. They were already followed to New Jefferson, so that would have been a dead giveaway. And with thousands of people in and out of National all day long, it was safer.

"Now look," Gary tells J.D., "this thing's got to go without a hitch, understand?"

"Gary," J.D. says, "have I ever let you down?"

"Yeah, well. Make sure the plane's ready. I have to wait here for Mandy to show up."

"Don't worry about it, big guy." J.D. flashes a smile and a thumbs-up, then walks to the back of the loading docks.

Gary stares hard down the access road, then at his watch. "Mandy, you're seventy-four minutes late," he says aloud.

Behind him, fast, nervous footsteps approach.

"She is still not here?" Ramón says. "She is *still* not here?"

He's been jumpy as a cat ever since Carla dropped him off this morning.

"And I see no cops. Where the hell are the cops?"

Gary lowers himself onto the edge of the loading dock, sits there like he doesn't have a thing on his mind except getting comfortable. "Well, if you could see 'em, Ramón, then your cousin Manny could see 'em, too, right?"

He shrugs.

"Don't worry," Gary adds. "They're out there."

"And where the hell is Amahnda? She was supposed to be here an hour and a half ago."

"There's still plenty of time. Go back to the hangar," Gary tells him. "You're the one who has to be there when Manny shows up. Because if you aren't, he's probably not going to stick around."

Ramón swallows hard and nods.

"Call me on the walkie-talkie when he shows," Gary says.

"What if she has not arrived yet with the papers?" he says. "What do we do then?"

"She'll be here, Ramón. Go back to the hangar."

He starts to protest, but then a jet roars above and eats his words. He gives up and goes back the way he came.

Ten minutes later the walkie-talkie crackles. "Arriving . . . he is arriving . . . Gary, he's early . . . do you hear me . . . what in hell am I supposed to . . ."

But Gary doesn't answer because a Jeep races up the road at the same time.

"She's here, Ramón. She's here. Now go tell your cousin you're fucking glad to see him. Over and out."

With the walkie-talkie in his pocket, Gary jumps the ten feet to the ground.

"Christ, Mandy, where in hell have you been?"

"Look," she says, "we need to talk. You won't believe—"

"Right now I'd believe just about anything." Gary reaches into her bag and pulls out the manila envelope.

"Gary . . ."

Another jet roars over their heads, and all he can see is her mouth moving. He kisses it, gives her J.D.'s thumbs-up, and takes the loading dock steps three at a time.

Outside the hangar, the rented Cessna sits nose to the runway. He sees the heat from the engines making waves in the air, zips up his coveralls, and pulls a hat down low on his forehead.

There's a black Caddy near the opposite side of the hangar, and Ramón's walking over to it like his feet are bare and he's walking on glass.

When he's a few feet away, one of the rear windows slides down about three inches. Then it goes up again and he starts walking back. Two guys get out of the Caddy. They could pass for any Friday night tag team Gary has ever seen.

"Manny says he wants to check out the plane. He is nervous. He wants a report from his own men that everything is kosher."

"Kosher?"

"That is what he said."

"Does he have the object?"

"In a box beside him on the seat."

"Okay. Tell them they walk through, they touch nothing, they get out. Understand?"

"They walk through," he repeats. "They touch nothing. They get out."

"Right." Gary pats him on the back.

Ramón stands there. His eyes are glazed. His lips have no blood in them.

"Hey. It's time to pull this off, Ramón. Are you okay?"

He nods. "Sure." He takes one deep breath and walks back to the Caddy.

Gary remembers the jumps he and Ramón made the day before. His standard jump class pitch didn't work. "Jumping out of a plane is a lot like having sex," Gary told him. "Almost everybody's nervous going in, but what happens while it's going on is so incredible, most people can't wait to try it again." But Ramón had more and more trouble, and he never made a solo jump. Gary is goddamn worried.

"Look," he's been telling Ramón all morning, "you have three things to remember. Step away from the plane. Watch your altimeter. Pull the cord at four thousand feet."

Across the hangar, Ramón manages to get the Schwarzenegger twins to the plane. Then he escorts one of them on board.

Gary approaches, but when he's about fifteen feet away, the bodyguard puts one hand in his pocket and the other one up like a traffic cop.

"I'm the pilot," Gary says. When he doesn't get a response, he tries again. "I fly the plane, and I need to get in there and do a pre-flight check, make sure everything works." He looks at his watch. "We're already behind schedule. I may have to cancel the flight."

One hand stays in his pocket, but the other one falls to his side.

Gary takes that as an okay.

Inside the plane, Ramón and the other twin are coming out of the rear compartment.

"We have a flight plan, you know," Gary says to Ramón, "and you're delaying it."

He heads for the cockpit, slides into the pilot's seat, and activates the control panel. Gary starts working the panel and making notes on a clipboard.

"Do you gentlemen have any questions about this flight?" he asks without turning around.

There's five seconds of silence, then Gary resumes checking gauges, flicking switches, and making phony notes, hoping to intimidate the novice fliers.

"Isn't there another passenger?" the talking twin asks.

"He boards when the pre-flight check's complete." Gary looks out the side window and sees J.D. standing with his arms crossed next to a luggage carrier. He's wearing a new hat, a new shirt and vest, and he's smoking a pipe.

"Okay," Gary says and waves at J.D. "I'm raising the boarding steps in five minutes."

The guard slowly backs out of the cockpit and joins his partner back at the Caddy.

Gary jumps up, tosses the clipboard, and steps out of the coveralls. It was something he and Mandy thought a lot about last night. What would a rich gringo buying Mayan artifacts wear? It took them three hours and four department stores to come up with identical outfits in J.D. and Gary's sizes. He brushes at the pants and shirt and thinks how good taste and a lot of money seem to go hand in hand.

J.D. comes through the door. "Did I do good?" he asks.

"You did real good." Gary takes his hat.

J.D. whistles. "You look real sharp. You want this, too?" He holds out the pipe.

"Keep it. And disappear fast."

Gary inserts the half-million-dollar envelope in the side pocket of the aisle seat facing the cockpit and reviews the seating plan. Ramón in the seat with the envelope. Manny in the window seat next to him. They'd gone over what they were going to do dozens of times.

"I'll come back after you have made your exchange," Gary told him. "You get up and go into the rear compartment and get into the chute."

That's when the problems are likely to start, he figures.

Back in the cockpit, Gary looks through the window to see a man, short and very wide, walking across the hangar. He's carrying a box in one hand and a briefcase in the other. He stops to say something to Ramón, who's patiently waiting at the foot of the steps.

The plane shifts a little under the weight as they board. Then Gary heads back to meet Manny.

"Mister ... ?" he asks.

"Manny," the fat man replies.

"Manny. Okay, I'm Guy Walker, and I'm interested in your, uh, item."

"Walker," he says. "Walker." He frowns. "Never heard the name."

"Well, I'm a very private collector." Gary smiles and offers his hand.

Manny shakes his head and holds up his hands, indicating the box and briefcase.

"Have a seat," Gary says, pointing to his assigned spot. "And Ramón."

He turns to pull up the steps and lock the door.

"Now, if you'll both fasten your seat belts until we're in the air. Then you two can conduct your business, and Manny and I will conduct ours after that."

"I don't get it," Manny says. "We're in the plane. We have the stuff. Why can't we do it now? And then get the hell out of here?"

Gary stiffens. "I only make deals in the air. Of course, if you want to call the whole thing off right now . . ." He points to the door.

Manny bends over as far as he can and drops the briefcase on the floor. He sets the box on his lap. "Forget the goddamn seat belt, none of them fit me anyway. Let's get this goddamn thing over with."

"I'll be back after you two are finished. I always like to be in the cockpit when we take off," Gary says. "Another idiosyncrasy."

Manny snorts and looks out the window. Gary catches Ramón's eye and nods in the direction of the side pocket of his seat. Ramón glances at the envelope, then nods.

Back in the cockpit, Gary asks for clearance and taxis away from the hangar. The sky is blue. But Gary notices a ridge of clouds moving in fast from the southwest, and realizes they don't have much time.

He heads east, for the flats, where there's no air traffic, and tops out at six thousand feet. He looks at his watch and decides to give them five more minutes. Ramón would have to be *quick*.

"Damn winds," Gary mutters. He sets it on autopilot and walks back to the cabin.

Ramón now has the briefcase on his lap, and the envelope with the half-million-dollar papers is on top of Manny's box.

"I suppose you want to do something with that," Gary says to Ramón. "Put it in a safe place, maybe? In the rear of the plane?"

Ramón licks his lips and tries to get up, but his seat belt's still fastened. He lets out a nervous chuckle and fumbles around in his lap.

"Besides, we might as well have a little privacy," Gary says to Manny.

"Privacy," Manny says. "Who cares up here? The birds?"

"Maybe the angels."

He frowns, looking like he doesn't want to hear talk about angels. "You've seen the papers," he says.

"I have."

With short, fat fingers he begins working on the box. He lifts out paper and bubble wrap, then holds it out in front of Gary.

"It belonged to a king," he says, gazing inside.

Gary hesitates, touching the statue. He's not quite sure if he can convince Manny he knows what he's doing. Then he recalls Ramón's words. "It's very valuable, very delicate, impossible to replace."

He decides to treat it like a Holley double pumper four-barrel carb. With that in mind, he has no trouble handling the Mayan dogs.

"I'll give you four for it," he says.

Manny's eyes narrow. "Four?"

"You don't think four million's a good enough offer?"

His eyes go very wide. "Four million?"

"Four and a half, then, but that's as high as I go. Take it or leave it."

He nods. "I'll take it."

"I'll have my man come by tomorrow to pick it up. He'll bring cash."

"Madre de Dios," Manny says.

Gary looks toward the rear compartment and decides it's time to check on Ramón.

"Excuse me," he says to Manny. "I'll get Ramón. Is he prone to air sickness? These small planes sometimes . . ."

"Nah," Manny interrupts. "Smooth as a limo." He smiles, suddenly looking like he's having a good time. "But go ahead, go ahead." He chuckles and looks out the window.

In the rear compartment, Ramón's in a jumpsuit, but without a parachute. The money is wrapped and on the floor.

"What in the hell are you doing?" Gary says. "We have a weather window here, remember? We've got five minutes and you're not even fucking ready!"

Ramón looks like he really does need the bathroom. He turns and walks into the tiny compartment, leaving Gary to package the cash and prep the parachute.

"Why should I jump?" he says when he comes out. "Take the plane down. Let the cops surround us. You think that fat pig's going to put up a fight?" He shakes his head. "I've lost everything already, and now you expect me to kill myself jumping out of this fucking plane. No way, man. No way."

"Ramón, listen to me, because I only have time to say this once." Gary begins putting on his own suit. "There are no cops, Ramón. That was only so you'd work with us. There's not going to be anybody waiting down there for you except Carla. No cops, Ramón. The money's yours. But it's only yours if you goddamn jump."

"You're fucking me."

"I'm fucking your cousin, Manny," Gary says. "We both are, you and me. All by ourselves."

Ramón leans toward Gary, and the look in his eyes isn't trust.

"So what the hell are you fucking him for?" he says.

"I'll tell you what I'm fucking him for. I'm fucking him for the government of the Yucatán peninsula." Gary has no idea where it came from, but he likes the sound of it.

The chips are falling into place behind Ramón's eyes. "Jesus," he says. "Jesus." He takes the chute and the bag with the money. "It's mine, the money?"

"For your trouble," Gary says. "Compliments of your cousin."

"I should have figured it out. I should have fucking known."

When they walk back into the main compartment, Manny's still looking out the window with a smile on his fat face. Gary releases the main door.

"What the fuck!" Manny yells.

"Adios primo." Ramón smiles at him and goes over

to the door. "Maybe now we are *mano a mano*. Even."
Then he stops, every muscle in his body tenses.

Five seconds, ten. "Step away, watch your altimeter,
pull the cord at four thousand feet," Gary tells him. He
gives him a shove, figuring the survival instinct will
kick in.

"What the fuck is going on?" Manny yells again.

"You ever fly a plane?" Gary asks.

"What are you talking about?"

"The thing is, once I jump, you'll be the only one
left. The cockpit's all yours, Manny. Have a nice landing."

Manny gets up and half runs toward the cockpit.
When he opens the door, he lets out a scream.

"Why?" he says. "Why are you doing this?"

Gary looks him over. "Because you're the one who
trashed my wife's house. She used to be a friend of
Ramón's. But then, she never did have very good taste
in men. I mean, she married me, right?"

That's when Manny reaches inside his jacket.

"You know what happens when you shoot a gun inside a plane?" Gary spreads his hands about two feet
apart, and then smacks them together. "Boom. The
whole thing goes up. Drop it, Manny, we have other options here."

"What? What are you talking about?"

"Drop the gun and find out."

It takes several seconds, but Manny finally drops the
gun.

"What do you want?" he asks. "Whatever you want,
you've got. Money to replace the things they broke.

Money for your trouble. Money to buy a new house. But don't jump. Don't fucking leave me here."

"Whatever I want?"

"Whatever you want."

Gary points to the statue and the papers. "Even those?"

"Those?"

"Fine. You keep 'em." Gary takes a step toward the door.

"No," he yells, "no. Here. They're yours."

"Didn't I tell you there were better options?"

He nods and hands over the box and envelope. "Better," he says, "much better."

Gary packs both items in a nylon bag. "And the gun, too," he says. "Just to be on the safe side."

The gun disappears into the bag, and Manny takes a step back.

"You know," Gary says, "I'm mad as hell about the house, but the real problem here is my dog, and that's something I'm having a hard time with."

"Your dog?" He looks like he's trying to understand a foreign language. "You want a new dog?"

"What I want is for you to piss in your pants." Gary steps nearer the door. "A word of advice, Manny. Never trust an angry guy in a parachute."

The last thing Gary sees before he jumps is Manny's face. It isn't a pretty sight.

CHAPTER TWENTY-SIX

It's always been guaranteed that any time I watch Gary jump, the wind's so strong that I know for sure it'll blow his parachute inside out and slam him into the ground at 120 miles an hour. Just like today.

Ringo lifts his nose and sniffs.

I keep telling myself that it's really just my perception of the wind getting mixed up with my anxiety. But it doesn't help. Never did.

A piece of charred celluloid blows across the toe of my shoe. Twenty-four prints, twenty-four negatives. Memories of my little trip with Ramón. I'd forgotten all about them until Carla tossed them on the car seat a couple of hours ago.

I walk away from the Jeep and look out across the flats, at the dust devils, then up at the plane making another slow circle in the sky, and wonder what he's waiting for. Tornadoes to form?

Then all of a sudden he's there, like a comma against the sky, and I start the old routine like it's been four days instead of four years.

One Mississippi, two Mississippi, three Mississippi,

four . . . I can feel my nails digging into my palms, and I know my teeth are clenched hard enough so my jaw's going to ache for days. But it's different this time. Maybe because he knows I'm watching, and for once, he remembers how much I hate free fall . . . five Mississippi, six . . . and then it opens, the chute, yellow and red and orange against the bright blue sky.

He comes closer and closer, as though he's aiming straight at me, and Ringo starts prancing. It's something Ringo learned early with Gary: to look up.

Gary would call it a pretty landing, a walk-away.

He comes toward us smiling, pulling the harness off with one hand, holding out a nylon bag to me with the other. Ringo lets out a few squeals.

I take the bag. "It worked? This is it?"

"I don't think it's something you'd want to put on the mantel," he says, "but still, careful you don't drop it."

Then all of a sudden there's the sound of engines behind us, and when I turn around, there's a line of cars coming up the road one after the other. They pull up all around us like Indians circling a wagon train.

"Holy shit," Gary says. He grabs me with one hand and wraps his harness around his other fist like a gladiator.

Ringo runs under the Jeep.

One man comes toward us, the others hang back. When he's a couple of feet away, he holds out his hand. "I'll take the bag," he says. "It does contain the stolen items?"

Gary backs us both away. "Who the hell are you?" he says.

B. Clinton has at least an inch and a half of clean white neck between the top of his collar and his hair, exactly the way I remembered. It's what convinced me to call him from the loading dock. I reminded myself that nobody has a neck like that unless he's a CPA or a fed.

"It's okay, Gary," I say. I hand B. Clinton the bag.

"Clinton," he says to Gary. "Bob Clinton." He flashes a badge under his lapel. "Customs." He looks at me. "Nice to see you again, Mrs. . . . Ms. Basch." He smiles and hands the bag off to someone else.

Gary's hold on me loosens a little.

"I called him, Gary," I say. "The other guys would have been following Manny to the airport, and they would have been waiting when you landed."

He lets go of me. "Who?"

"The people who broke into my house, hurt Ringo, shot that kid." I sigh. "Would you like me to tell you about my day?"

"You mean it wasn't Manny? He wasn't responsible for any of that?"

I shake my head.

The plane drones above us, and we all look up.

"Jesus Christ," Gary says, "you mean I made the guy piss in his pants for nothing?"

As we're watching, the plane's wings dip to one side, then the other, which mean's J.D.'s out of the locker and at the controls.

"Don't waste your time feeling sorry for him," B. Clinton says. "He's in illegal treasures up to his neck. Only this time that neck would have ended up broken. Believe me, given his choices of a welcoming committee at the airport, he'd choose us hands down."

Gary looks at him. "And who is this other committee you're talking about?"

"The international cartel the artifact was marked for. They tend to get very unhappy when outsiders invade their turf. Manny Rodriguez stumbled into one of their more lucrative arrangements. We suspected Ramón had cut himself a piece of that same dangerous pie," he slides his eyes onto me, "and had possibly involved you." He puts his hands on his hips and stretches his back, makes a face as though it hurts. "We had intended," he says, "to keep you under surveillance." He frowns. "But that turned out to be a little harder than we expected."

"It was *you* following us?" Gary says.

"From time to time. Our men seem to think car washes only work one way. And as far as I know, none of them can fly." For a second he almost looks as though he's going to smile, then he wipes his hand across his mouth. "You know, you could have gotten yourselves killed."

"It kept crossing our minds," Gary says. "Which reminds me." He zips open a pocket on the leg of his jump suit and pulls out a gun. Everyone except me and B. Clinton takes a step back. "Thought I should relieve Manny of this before I jumped." He smiles. "For J.D.'s sake."

"Thanks," B. Clinton says, taking it.

"What about Manny's bodyguards at the airport?" Gary asks.

"In custody."

Gary nods. Then he grabs my arm. "What about Ramón? Did you see his chute open?"

"It opened," I tell him, "I saw it open."

"Good and early?"

"Good and early."

That seems to make him happy.

"We have people picking him up," B. Clinton says.

That seems to make Gary unhappy.

Another car arrives. Someone gets out and comes running up to us. "The other guy's missing," he says. "We followed the directions to the pickup site, and we waited by the van. A Ryder van, right?"

B. Clinton looks at me.

I nod. "Ryder. Yes."

"But no one showed. When we checked it out, there were ramps inside, and tracks like somebody backed a car out."

B. Clinton looks at Gary, who shrugs, then he looks at me. "She tell you she had other plans?"

I shake my head. "We didn't talk a lot."

"According to your plan, what was she supposed to do after she picked him up?"

Gary and I look at each other. "I don't think we got that far," Gary says. "We were kind of playing it by ear."

B. Clinton groans. "Isn't there a sum of money involved somewhere in this thing?"

"Something of a sum," Gary says. "Something like half a million."

"So where is it?"

Gary looks like he hates what he's going to say. "It sort of developed into a situation where, before I knew what happened, Ramón and the money had jumped."

"You let him take the money?" I say.

"No way! It's just that one minute he was there and the next he was gone," Gary replies.

B. Clinton looks out toward the flats. He shakes his head.

"They just found his chute," someone yells from the car.

"That's *my* chute," Gary says, "and I'd like it back."

B. Clinton looks at him. "You'll get it back eventually." He sighs. "We'll need you both to come in later. For statements." The cars start to leave one at a time. "We advise against people who don't know what they're doing getting involved in things like this. Maybe now you know why." He starts to walk off, stops. "By the way, the government of Mexico is always grateful for the return of its national treasures, so when you come in to give your statements, there'll probably be some kind of reward." He smiles.

We watch him walk away.

"Reward?" I say.

Gary puts his arm around my shoulder. "Don't get too excited. It's probably a replica of the national treasure they're getting back." He smiles and gives me a hug. "You did pretty damn good, Amanda Basch."

I hug him back. "You did pretty damn good yourself."

By the time we've bagged his parachute and coaxed Ringo out from under the Jeep, the wind's a low, constant moan.

We stand there for a while, letting it blow at us.

"Do you feel it?" Gary asks.

"Feel what?"

"The positive ions. They're supposed to make you feel exhilarated, maybe even a little crazy."

I lean toward him. "And how would you be able to tell?"

"Funny," he says, "very funny."

"So what do you think happened to Ramón?"

He shrugs, frowns. "I was just wondering if maybe he did back a car out of it. A Maserati, maybe?"

Out on the flats, the dust is blowing in circles.

"I can't believe Ramón did it," I say, "that he had the balls to grab the money and jump like that."

"Well, actually, it didn't go quite that way."

I look at him.

"The guy went catatonic, Mand. He needed something big enough to jump for."

"So you handed him half a million dollars?"

He bends down, unzips the pocket on the leg of his jumpsuit, says something I can't hear.

"Huh?"

He takes out a nylon bag. "I said, it was more like half of a half." He shrugs. "Maybe a little less."

I look at the bag. I look at him. "You're kidding." I'm in shock.

"Hey," he says, "we went to a lot of trouble."

We stand there with the wind whipping around us, looking at each other. We both smile at the same time. "C'mon," I say, "let's go home. We'll figure out what to do with the money later."

We get into the Jeep, and I turn it around, get back on the road.

"You know what I was thinking about up there?" he asks after a while.

I shake my head.

"I was thinking about your friend the CPA."

"You were thinking about Carter?"

"Well, not about him exactly, but about the world ending. Like what if it was going to happen tonight?"

A gust of wind hits the side of the Jeep, and for a second, it feels as though we're going sideways, then all of a sudden it's gone.

"C'mon, Gary. It's weird enough coming from Carter, but it's really weird coming from you."

"Just say it was going to happen." He wipes a streak of dust off the dashboard and looks at it on his finger. "Who would you want to be with when it did?"

I grip the steering wheel a little tighter, in case we get pushed sideways again. "Ringo," I say.

"Besides Ringo."

"My mother."

"Besides your mother."

"Well, who would you want to be with?"

"You," he says, without hesitating for even a second. "And if you wouldn't want to be with me, that's okay. I'd still want to be with you."

"Well, if I didn't want to be with you, but you wanted to be with me, then you'd have a problem, right?"

"I could wear a disguise," he says. "I could put on your mother's clothes and dye my hair blue."

"Or you could pretend you really didn't want to be with me, that you just wanted to be with Ringo, and since I know that Ringo would want to be with you, too, then I'd have to let you stay."

"Or I could dangle my watch in front of your eyes and hypnotize you. Get you to believe you really wanted me there."

"Or you could get me to believe that I really wanted you there without hypnotizing me."

I feel him looking at me. "And how would I do that?"

"Just by saying you wanted to be with me till the end of the world."

He clears his throat. "I thought I was saying that."

"Say it again."

"I want to be with you, Amanda, until the end of the world."

I pull over and stop, because what's happening is serious enough to require all my attention. "Okay," I say, looking straight ahead at the road. "Now ask me."

He undoes his seat belt and turns toward me. "Okay, who would you want to be with if the world was going to end tonight?"

"You." I turn and look at him.

"You're sure? You're not just saying it because I said it?"

"It's not the kind of thing you say just to be polite. I'm sure. I'm very sure."

He puts his hand on my cheek. Ringo sighs in the backseat. The wind slams the side of the Jeep again and whistles through the canvas top. And somewhere out in that same wind, I picture a red Maserati carrying Ramón and Carla and half of half a million dollars far, far away.

Meet "Dutch" O'Brien,
a p.i. for fans of Kinsey Millhone, in

BUCK NAKED
by Joyce Burditt

Demeter "Dutch" O'Brien is a p.i. consulting on the television series *Stone, Private Eye*. The show's fading star, Buck Stevens, is a lustful sixty-something with a taste for minors.

For a glimpse of Dutch and BUCK NAKED, please read on. . . .

Buck Stevens saw that the whole crew was watching him. "What the hell you looking at?" He grunted and moved toward the stage door. "I'll be in my trailer. Don't nobody bother me."

As Buck slammed the stage door behind him the crew exhaled a sigh of relief. Compared with most days, Buck was in a great mood.

Personally, I find Buck's antics more entertaining than his television show, a lumpy blend of down-home hokum and mysteries that often don't make any sense. Before being hired on the show, I'd never watched it— and I'd said so when the producers offered me the job.

They didn't seem offended or even surprised, maybe because they thought private investigators never watch television or more likely because they watched it themselves only when they had to. But ten minutes after I accepted the job, a messenger arrived with twenty-two tapes and a note "suggesting" that familiarizing myself with the series might be "helpful."

I watched all twenty-two and discovered that *Stone, Private Eye* concerned a private investigator who works out of his home in Sassafras, Arkansas, and that most of his clients are his Sassafras neighbors or folks passing through Sassafras just long enough to be murdered—or occasionally an outsider, when a big enough star could be coaxed by money or sweet-talked by Buck into playing the part. Each episode begins with a murder that Sam Stone investigates by ambling all over town— dropping in at the barbershop, filling station, and the Koffee Kup Diner—where he asks foxy questions and dispenses folksy advice. Somewhere along the way he solves a friend's personal problem, such as a buddy whose hens aren't laying until Buck changes the radio station in the henhouse and gives those Rhode Island Reds the Dolly Parton they've been craving instead of that "big city rock 'n' roll crap." Then along toward the end of each episode Buck gets a hot idea, usually while sitting alone in his kitchen. He jumps up and yells "I got it!" then runs off, solves the murder, and nabs the killer. Cut to commercial, tune in next week.

Watching twenty-two episodes has taught me three things. All the shows are the same. Under no circumstances, unless I have a burning desire to be murdered or jailed, will I ever set foot in Sassafras, Arkansas. *Stone, Private Eye* is the cure for insomnia.

On nights when my nerves scream like a cheap car

alarm and I toss, haunted by Michael, I slip a tape into the machine, watch Buck amble for ten or twelve minutes, and am dulled into a drift that's almost sleep. Sometimes, dull is comforting, even necessary. Dull soothes the soul. Dull quiets the mind. Dull heals the body. Late at night I know I've made the right choice. I've picked the right job. Because nowhere else will I find a world as predictably, resolutely, unrelentingly dull as *Stone, Private Eye*. I know I've lucked out and keep watching.

Of course, that's an opinion I keep to myself. Though most people who work on the show would agree, no one dares even to think it, for fear Buck will read something less than worship in their eyes. Buck demands worship. Buck demands groveling. Buck demands stuff Buck hasn't thought of yet. Buck may not know what he wants, but he does know that if he doesn't get it, he'll fire every last son of a bitch and good riddance. The show might be turgid but the set is a circus where, at any given moment and for no reason at all, the ringmaster can get pissed and set the tigers on the crowd. Diverting.

It's been three months since I checked into an upscale loony bin that promised "safe and effective drug withdrawal in a supportive setting." Had a nice ring to it, like the "friendly skies." Good thing I never buy into ads. Just as the "friendly skies" are mined with turbulence and wind shear (but the quickest route from one place to another), the loony bin was the shortcut from dying to living. I ignored the "supportive setting" and got down to business—sweating, shaking, insomnia, nightmares. Curled up on my bed, I dared it to kill me. A shrink dropped in and advised me to cry. Standard shrink rap. I told her that you don't cry about the things

you do to yourself. Then, just to be ornery, I told her that the next time I try to destroy myself I'll cut to the chase—Russian roulette. Click, click, *bang*, Forest Lawn.

I should have kept my mouth shut. She freaked.

Now the shrink, eminent Beverly Hills psychiatrist Dr. Karen O'Brien, who's also my mother, is convinced that I need an extended stay at her psychiatric facility. Her husband, Dunn Carlisle, who was bred on a stud farm for the purpose of servicing Mother, thinks I need to get laid. Dr. Morris Spellman, the shrink assigned to me by Mother at her dingbat emporium, has concluded that I need to see him every Monday, Wednesday, and Friday for the rest of my life. I've written to the president, soliciting his sage advice, but as yet he hasn't replied. When he does, I'll take all these options under advisement and the winner will receive an all-expenses-paid trip to Death Valley, plus a pair of my baby shoes, bronzed.

The truth is I'm done with destroying myself. My brain on drugs (sizzle, sizzle) accomplished what no broken heart can do. I forgot who I was.

My name is Demeter "Dutch" O'Brien. I'm female, thirty-one and a third, five feet seven, one hundred and twenty-four pounds, dark brown hair, green eyes, no distinguishing marks I care to talk about—and I was last seen skipping down the Yellow Brick Road.

I was, and will be again when I choose, a private detective.

I'm licensed to carry a gun, which I do, in a shoulder holster cradled just beneath my heart.